Antonia kissed the doll's no

d Antonia shuffle

he closet door and

ong that sounded

Hush-a-bye and good night
Till the bright morning light
Takes the sleep from your eyes
Hush-a-bye, baby bright.

She sighed, shut the door, and dove back under her covers. It didn't take long for her teeth to start grinding together. It made my own teeth hurt listening to it, but I knew snoring would follow soon enough. But that night, while I waited for her rumbling snore, I heard something else.

"Good night, Lucy, sleep tight."

I pulled the covers back from my head and looked at Antonia. She was revving up her snoring. I glanced at the closet door. It was shut tight.

I shivered and pulled the covers back over my head. It didn't make sense. Antonia was never one to talk in her sleep. But that wasn't the strangest part. I figured it was just my imagination, but I could have sworn I heard those words coming from inside the closet . . .

HUSH-A-BYE

OTHER BOOKS YOU MAY ENJOY

HUSH-A-BYE

JODY LEE MOTT

VIKING

VIKING
An imprint of Penguin Random House LLC, New York

First published in the United States of America by Viking,
an imprint of Penguin Random House LLC, 2021
First paperback edition published 2022

Visit us online at penguinrandomhouse.com.

THE LIBRARY OF CONGRESS HAS CATALOGED THE HARDCOVER EDITION AS FOLLOWS:
Names: Mott, Jody Lee, author. Title: Hush-a-bye / Jody Lee Mott.
Description: New York : Viking, 2021. | Audience: Ages 8–12 | Audience: Grades 7–9
Summary: "Lucy and her younger sister find a broken doll that has astonishing
powers and a sinister agenda"—Provided by publisher.
Identifiers: LCCN 2021018690 (print) | LCCN 2021018691 (ebook) ISBN 9780593206782
(hardcover) | ISBN 9780593206799 (paperback) | ISBN 9780593206805 (epub)
Subjects: CYAC: Supernatural—Fiction. | LCGFT: Paranormal fiction.
Classification: LCC PZ7.1.M6787 Hu 2021 (print) | LCC PZ7.1.M6787 (ebook)
DDC [Fic]—dc23 LC record available at https://lccn.loc.gov/2021018690
LC ebook record available at https://lccn.loc.gov/2021018691

Paperback ISBN 9780593206799

Printed in the United States of America

1st Printing

LSCH

Design by Jim Hoover   Text set in Minion Pro

HUSH-A-BYE

1

IT WAS DEEP in the afternoon of the last Tuesday of summer when I kicked away a willow branch lying on the riverbank and found the head.

My eyes had been closed. I'd been imagining, for no particular reason, how the September sun would look to the salamanders trolling the murky Susquehanna riverbed. Like margarine on burnt toast, I supposed. Then my foot knocked into the branch, my eyes opened, and another eye stared back at me.

Its yellow hair was tangled with twigs and muck and broken glass like some crazy bird's nest. It had a scratched cheek, a chipped-up nose, and a grimy clot of mud in the hole where the left eye should have been. I picked up the head and held it by its ragged neck. The body, I supposed, had long since floated away.

"Poor little doll," I said. "Where'd the rest of you go?"

I glanced behind me. My sister, Antonia, was somewhere along the slope above the bank, searching for flat rocks to skip on the water. She was always somewhere close by.

I bent down to drop the head back in the hollow space where it must have been hiding for weeks—maybe years, for all I knew. I wondered if the rest of her might be hiding somewhere on the small river island that sat a couple hundred feet out from where I stood. The curve of its shore matched the curve of the riverbank like a puzzle piece, and it was covered in tall birch trees that jostled against each other.

I looked at the river. Bars of light shivered across the surface. There hadn't been a single cloud in the sky since the middle of August. Nothing above us but a wide sheet of blue.

Looking across ripples of sunlight on the river's brown face, I wondered what would happen if I tossed the doll's head into the water. I wanted to make the sunlight dancing there smash into a million pieces. Somehow, that seemed like the best possible thing I could do that day.

I weighed the doll's head dangling from my hand, its hair twisted in my fingers. Its one good eye watched me. Almost like my daddy's eyes—bright emerald green and full of mischief. At least, that's how I remembered them.

I bit my lip and swallowed the sour ball of pain rising up my throat. The eye still looked at me, but it didn't seem so bright anymore. It was dull and scratched and looked like nothing more than a cheap glass eye stuck in a poor broken doll's head.

"Lucy?"

I turned. Antonia stood there with her hands cupped together, full of rocks too fat for anything but sinking with a loud plop. She was smiling, and her eyes were wide open even though she was facing into the sun. I could never understand how she was able to do that without squinting. The sparkly duckling barrette she'd worn since second grade glittered in the sunlight.

"Gross," Antonia said, but she was still smiling. "What's that?"

"Nothing," I said. "Just an old doll's head. Come look."

Antonia dropped the rocks, letting them thump in the undergrowth, and shuffled toward me. I pressed my finger against the doll's cheek.

"See?" I said. "Only an old broken doll's head." Antonia wrapped her hand around the head and tried to pull it toward her. I jerked it away.

"Stop that," I said, a little more harshly than I'd intended. "There's glass in its hair. You'll cut yourself. I'm going to throw it back where I found it. Nothing but trash anyway."

Antonia pouted. I tried to ignore her, but that pout always rankled me. Even though there was only a year's difference between us, sometimes Antonia acted like such a baby. According to Mom, Antonia just had her own "Antonia way" of doing things, which meant she needed a little extra help at school, and a little more patience from me. I knew it wasn't completely her fault why she acted the way she did, so I tried to be understanding. I didn't always succeed.

I shook my head to break up the annoyed feeling. There were still a few more hours of this day to enjoy my freedom.

No sense in ruining that with fussing over things I couldn't change. And no sense in keeping some dirty, broken, good-for-nothing doll's head.

I stepped toward the river and drew my arm back. A gust of wind shook the gray birch branches across the far bank. As they swayed, I thought I heard something—a faint voice whispering among the sound of rattling dry leaves.

Take me home.

I swung about and glared at my sister. "What did you say?"

Antonia cocked her head to one side. "I didn't say nothing. Must have been the doll."

I looked at my sister for a long time, then shook my head. "Don't be silly." I picked shards of glass out of the doll's hair. Too many worries about school tomorrow were making me jumpy, making me hear things. I needed to settle myself down.

"It's sad, though, don't you think?" I said. "Poor thing left all alone here. Her little body's probably washed all the way to China."

"My teacher read a book about a glass bunny that got lost," Antonia said. "He got drowned in the ocean until some fisherman pulled him out and saved him."

"Probably shouldn't throw her back in the river. That would be littering. We can put her in the trash when we get back home."

Antonia leaned in and squinted at the doll's head. "She's not garbage," she said. "She needs us. She's lonely." She rested her cheek on my arm. "Can't we take her back to the trailer? We can fix her up, and maybe we can find another body for her."

I nudged Antonia away. "Mom wouldn't like it. She's already threatened to take a shovel to all the junk under your bed."

"It's not junk," Antonia said. "They're my precious treasures."

Her precious treasures were a flat soccer ball, a trunkless stuffed elephant named Mr. Lumps, a large bag full of knotted rubber bands, a papier-mâché Earth with only five continents, and about a hundred other bits and pieces she'd picked up here and there and shoved under her bed "for later."

"She'd be the most precious treasure of all," Antonia said. She nestled her cheek against my arm again and fluttered her eyelashes. "Please, can we keep her? Pretty please?"

I had to smile. She knew her eyelash flutter always worked on me. "I suppose so . . . if we don't tell Mom."

Antonia's eyes grew wide. "You mean lie?"

The doll's green eye glowed in the afternoon light, and the sound of the river filled our ears. A single cloud, thin as a whisper, floated just above the treetops.

"Not a lie." I trailed my pinkie across the doll's stubbed nose. "A secret. *Our* secret."

2

I'D COME DOWN to the river almost every summer day since we moved to Oneega Valley, a long, narrow ribbon of town in New York State, just a few miles north of Pennsylvania. Antonia had found the dirt footpath hidden under a row of winterberry bushes running behind our trailer. You had to squeeze through them, shuffle sideways down the path to avoid the pricker bushes and stinging nettles that grew between the willows, then slide down a low slope to get to the riverbank.

Antonia had summer school, so I usually went alone. I'd sit on the bank under a willow tree for hours, watching the dragonflies dance across the water and the island's birch trees nod in the wind. Dark columns poked up here and there between the pale gray trees like a giant's fingers. I liked to imagine they were the remains of a long-forgotten meeting house of some secret society. I dreamed about visiting it one day to get a better look at those columns, but the river was too muddy for swimming, and we didn't have a boat.

It was strange I'd never noticed the doll's head all those days and weeks I'd spent there. Not until Antonia showed up, anyway. That figured. I mean, I liked her company, but things always got more complicated with her around. And now here we were heading back home, trying to sneak in a busted-up doll's head.

After Antonia and I squeezed through the winterberry bushes, we spotted Mom's baby-blue junker parked between the trailer and the tall ginkgo tree. We weren't expecting to see her so soon. Then again, we were never too sure when we'd see Mom, day or night.

"Don't say anything about the head," I reminded Antonia as we approached the trailer. Her eyes grew wide, like I'd said the most unbelievable thing she'd ever heard.

"I wasn't going to." As if she wasn't the biggest blabber-mouth in the world.

"Well, just remember it," I said, and shooed her on ahead.

Antonia slumped her chin on her chest and pouted. "I *said* I wasn't going to."

Mom lay on our old, beat-up couch with the faded bird-of-paradise slipcover. A damp washcloth covered her eyes, and her smudged sneakers were still tied tightly on her feet. That meant a bad day at work.

"Hey there, firecrackers," she said in a gravelly voice, not taking off the washcloth. Antonia knelt on the floor near Mom's head. She removed her duckling barrette and leaned back so Mom could stroke her fine, straight hair.

It seemed like Antonia got all the best parts from our parents—Mom's glossy chocolate-brown hair and dark eyes, and Daddy's high cheekbones—while I ended up with a dirty-blond mess that ate combs, a pug nose, and eyes the color of dishwater.

At least neither one of us ended up with our daddy's temper. We'd already had our fill of it anyway. Not anymore, though, or at least not in the twelve months since we'd last seen him.

I carefully tucked my bag out of sight at the other end of the couch. Mom raised her feet to let me sit down. I pulled off her sneakers and socks and rubbed her feet.

"Mmm, that feels good, Peppernose," she said. Mom called me that because of the dark freckles all over my fish-belly-white face. I thought they made me look ugly, but I still liked the name. She only ever used it at home, so it was like our own secret code.

I trailed my finger across the calla lily tattoo that curled along her calf. "Work go okay?" I asked.

Mom shrugged. "It went."

Antonia and I exchanged a worried look. I hated how tired she sounded after work, and how her clothes always smelled like onions and cheap coffee.

She worked weird hours as a waitress at Theodora's Hometown Diner. Mornings, evenings, weekends, holidays— there wasn't a time or a day she wouldn't be expected to show up. She never talked about her job except to say it was like trying to juggle ten balls while tap-dancing, and every once in a while someone would throw you a watermelon and a bag of cats.

"We were down by the river," Antonia blurted out. Whenever she gets worried about Mom, she rattles her mouth about random things no one asked her. I shot her a look before she blabbed everything about the doll head. "Oh yeah," she went on, winking at me, "but we didn't find anything there." Like Mom wouldn't see right through her.

Sure enough, Mom lifted a corner of the washcloth and squinted at Antonia. "What did you find, and where did you put it?" Antonia once brought home a pail full of tadpoles. She'd put them under her bed and promptly forgot about them until a week passed and their death-stink got Mom's attention.

"Just some skipping stones," I said quickly, before Antonia could mess things up even more. "She wanted to bring some home, but I made her leave them there."

That seemed to satisfy Mom. She lowered the washcloth and handed her foot back to me.

"Looking forward to the first day of school tomorrow?" she asked me. *Looking forward?* Icy fingers dug into my gut.

"Sure," I lied.

"Keep an eye on your sister as much as you can. Oh, and I called the school today and asked if Antonia could have lunch with you on her first day."

I squeezed my mom's foot. She yelped. "Ow, watch it there," she said.

"Lunch?" The icy fingers curled into a fist. "With me? And all the other seventh graders?"

"Can I sit with you and your friends?" Antonia squealed.

"No!" I shouted, a lot louder than I meant to. Mom lifted the washcloth and stared at me. Antonia pouted. I looked down like I'd suddenly found something interesting under my fingernails. "I mean, why doesn't she go with the other sixth graders?"

"Lucille Penelope Bloom," Mom said. I winced. Once she trotted out my full name, I knew I was sunk. "It's just for one day. You know how flustered Antonia gets with new situations. I don't think it too much to ask to let her sit with you for a half hour out of the first day of school."

"It's forty-two minutes," I mumbled.

"Fine. Forty-two minutes, then."

"And she'll be with me on the bus."

Mom swung her legs out and took hold of my chin. Not painfully, but firmly. "Are we going to have a problem here?"

Whenever Mom did this, I knew she meant business. Not that she'd ever hurt me, like you saw with some parents. Besides, I never pushed too hard. I just couldn't do it. I shook my head.

Mom smiled and pulled me into a hug. Antonia squeezed against her on the other side.

"I'm not trying to make things hard for you, Peppernose," she said. "I just want to make sure both my girls get through middle school without too much trouble. Okay?"

"No trouble on the double," Antonia said, and giggled.

"Double trouble is right," Mom said. "Why don't you two go to your room and see what I got for you to wear for your first day back?"

Antonia gasped. "New clothes?"

Mom sighed. "Well, they were on clearance." Antonia didn't care. She bolted off to our room with her howler-monkey yell on full volume.

Mom nudged me with her shoulder. "You too, big sister. Check out what I got for you. I think you'll like it."

"No stripes?" I asked.

Mom shook her head and lay back down, covering her eyes with the washcloth. "No stripes. You think I just met you yesterday?"

I started to walk away, then stopped and turned back. The icy fist pounded my gut. *Just tell her*, I thought. *If she knows, maybe she'll let you stay home. Just for one day. Maybe a week. Or a year.*

"Mom?"

"Yeah, Peppernose?"

I opened my mouth to say one thing, then shut it tight and opened it again. "Thanks for the clothes."

Mom waved a limp hand. "Anything for my firecrackers. Now git."

I wasn't two steps into the bedroom when Antonia snatched away my backpack and nearly tore off my arms.

"Watch it!" I complained, but she was already focused on pulling out the doll's head. Our closet door was open, and it was clear Antonia had been busy setting up a place of honor on top of a cardboard box she'd shoved inside.

"Perfect," she said, and kissed the doll's nose as she set it on the box. Then from a corner of our room she dragged a little wooden chair Mom had picked up from a yard sale years ago and set it facing the doll head.

"I don't think that's a good idea," I said. "Mom's going to find that thing and throw it in the trash. Hide it in the dresser."

Antonia shook her head. "Can't."

"Why not?"

Antonia rolled her eyes. "How can I have conversations with her through the dresser? That's so rude." Then she squeezed her behind in the tiny chair built for a much tinier behind than she'd had for some time and shut the closet door. And that, apparently, was the end of that.

Later that night, when the lights were out and the covers were pulled over my head, I heard Antonia shuffle out from her bed. She tapped lightly on the closet door and slid it open. And then she whispered a song that sounded kind of familiar.

> *Hush-a-bye and good night*
> *Till the bright morning light*

Takes the sleep from your eyes
Hush-a-bye, baby bright

She sighed, shut the door, and dove back under her covers. It didn't take long for her teeth to start grinding together. She did it every night, and it sounded like she was chewing on a brick. One of these nights, she was going to grind her teeth down to the gums. It made my own teeth hurt listening to it, but I knew snoring would follow soon enough. It was still annoying, but at least I could sleep through it. But that night, while I waited for her rumbling snore, I heard something else.

"Good night, Lucy, sleep tight."

I pulled the covers back from my head and looked at Antonia. She'd already stopped grinding and was revving up her snoring. I glanced at the closet door. It was shut tight.

I shivered and pulled the covers back over my head. It didn't make sense. Antonia was never one to talk in her sleep. But that wasn't the strangest part. I figured it was just my imagination, but I could have sworn I heard those words coming from inside the closet.

3

"LUCY, LOOK! I think I see one falling. Do you see? Do you see?" Antonia danced about in an early-morning quilt of sunlight and shadow as she strained to look through the branches of the ginkgo tree.

"It's only the beginning of September." I shifted my back-pack to get a better look. The fan-shaped leaves were still summer green. "Too soon."

A year ago, when we first moved into the trailer, we discovered the best thing about our new home was the tall ginkgo tree growing next to it. The only trees we'd had at our previous house were a couple of sour-looking crab apples. It had been near the end of October, so Antonia and I had started planning the leaf-pile stunts we'd do once the leaves fell. We waited and waited almost the whole fall for the leaves to drop off the ginkgo tree. As the days and weeks went by, most of the other trees had shed their leaves bit by bit until they were bare as skeletons, but not the ginkgo. Its leaves didn't budge, not a single one. Not even late in November.

Then, one morning, a few days after the Thanksgiving break, we stumbled out of our trailer to catch the school bus and discovered a neat circle of leaves around the trunk of the ginkgo. Its branches were completely bare. Somehow, they'd all fallen off overnight at exactly the same time.

This year, I hoped we'd get lucky and they'd all drop right when we looking at it. But it was the first day back to school, so I didn't feel particularly lucky about anything.

I tugged on the strap of Antonia's bulging backpack, the pink kitten one she'd had since third grade.

"The bus'll be coming," I said. "I don't want to be late."

Antonia moaned, then tromped on toward the stop. I could see her straps were getting so frayed, I wondered if they'd hold. It looked like she'd jammed in several of her precious treasures along with her school supplies. As long as she didn't bring the doll's head. That would be a step too far into Weirdville, even for Antonia.

Despite my warnings that morning, the duckling barrette still clung stubbornly to her head. She may as well have worn a KICK ME sign. I wanted to be her protector, but my qualifications for that job were pretty thin. She'd be on her own in middle school. The barrette was not a good start. I know it sounds mean, but sometimes I wished her brain was wired better.

Even worse, there were some days I wished I didn't even have a sister.

Our bus stop was the second one on the route. So, like always, I grabbed the safe seat right behind the bus driver. Antonia jammed herself next to me, but I didn't mind. She didn't know it, but she was helping me. With her there, I could sit by the window and not worry about who might plop next to me.

The icy fingers in my belly unclenched a little. Antonia slipped her backpack to the floor and craned her neck over the seat to spy down the back of the bus.

"This doesn't look any different from my old bus," she said, sounding a little disappointed.

"All buses are the same," I said in a quiet voice.

"What?" Antonia shouted, and whipped her head about. On the opposite seat, a sliver-thin blond boy with a finger halfway up his nose squinched his eyes at her. I rapped Antonia's thigh with the back of my hand.

"Stop yelling," I whispered.

Antonia shot me a puzzled look, then folded her arms and slumped in her seat. "I thought it was going to be bigger."

The next two minutes passed quietly. The only sounds were the rumble of the bus, the wheezy breathing of the little blond boy, and Antonia picking her teeth with her thumb.

Two whole minutes.

I tried to lose myself in those minutes, like it was the last piece of time left in the world. If I ever got to heaven, and it turned out to be nothing more than a rattling bus ride with a skinny nose picker and my sister sucking at her teeth over and over again for eternity, I'd be okay with that.

But happiness would have to wait. I was heading to middle school.

Once the bus cleared the trailer park, the houses grew bigger, the evenly mowed lawns gleamed greener, and the number of rust-bucket cars like ours dwindled considerably.

Soon the bus squealed to halt, the door whooshed open, and a noisy pack of kids piled on. They all walked past Antonia and me. Most ignored us. A few made faces. None of them said hello. Neither did I.

Antonia didn't seem to notice or care. She was too busy petting the red panda on her shirt. But then Gus Albero, a big lump of a boy who was always tearing up the streets on his dirt bike, thumped up the bus steps. His weasel-faced friend Zoogie slinked and snickered close behind. He gave Gus a hard shove, and Gus, not expecting it, lost his balance and tipped forward. His hands slammed hard against the corner of our seat, and the vibrations shot straight up through my spine.

I stopped breathing and waited. *Please, please, please, please go away*, my brain pleaded. My body did nothing at all. Like usual.

But not Antonia. She shoved Gus back with both hands. "Watch out, jerk!" she said.

Gus stared at her for a second like he couldn't figure out what spaceship she'd just beamed down from. Then he snorted and said, "Smell you later." But he still backed off.

Now it was my turn to stare at Antonia. I couldn't believe how easily she'd done that. Most of the time I was embarrassed how Antonia "had her filters off," like Mom would say. She'd just blurt out whatever rolled through her brain at any given moment, usually the worst possible one. Like the time in the grocery store parking lot when Antonia gawked at a very large woman with low-riding pants wrestle a fifty-pound bag of dog food into the back of her VW Bug.

"Mom," she'd said in a shout you could hear halfway across the lot, "you see that lady showing her big butt? I bet you could stick a couple of quarters in there like a gumball machine."

I'd never known my mom's face could turn that shade of red.

But this was different. The way Antonia handled Gus was excellent. Maybe the day wouldn't be so bad after all. Maybe having Antonia act as a buffer at lunch could actually work. She'd say all the things I never dared to say.

The icy fingers wiggled free a little. I may have even smiled.

Then the bus jerked to stop at the corner of Main and Little, and the bus doors whooshed open once again. A pair of hard heels *click-click-click*ed up the steps. A whiff of cherry and cinnamon tickled the air.

My smile, if it ever was there, vanished.

Madison Underwood appeared, filling the aisle like a rolling thunderhead. And those icy fingers reached up through my throat, clamped on my brain, and dragged it down to my stomach.

Madison—Maddie to her friends—was as flashy and polished as a new bicycle. Her rosy skin, straight white teeth, and glossy nails gleamed, and her smooth black hair flowed easily over her shoulders. Everyone looked at her, including me, and she knew it. Her eyes soaked up all the adoration.

But when those copper-brown eyes found mine, the pleasure drained away, and all that was left was pure poison. All for me.

"Keep moving there, honey," the bus driver said. Madison gave me a half second's worth of eye venom, then turned to the bus driver and smiled.

"Sorry, Mrs. Hamish," Madison said in her sugary, finger-wrapping voice. Mrs. Hamish, like every other adult, returned her smile. Madison breezed down the aisle, followed by her giggling twin minions, Ashley and Gretta Oslo.

As the trio passed, I let out the breath I'd been holding. It was over. The worst moment of the morning bus ride, the one I'd been dreading and trying not to think about was over. There'd be other bad moments waiting for me at school, but at least I could check this one off the list.

That's what I told myself. And like usual, I was wrong.

"Wow, she's pretty as a lollipop," Antonia said. Very loudly.

I stiffened, feeling the scorch of Madison's stare as she took in the loud girl with the sparkly duckling barrette and the clearance-aisle red-panda shirt. The one sitting next to me.

"Hi, I'm Antonia," my sister continued, answering a question no one had asked. "I'm Lucy's sister."

My throat clenched tight. I wanted to reach out and grab Antonia by the neck and shake her until her brains rattled, screaming *Shut up! Shut up!* I couldn't have done it, though. In fact, that would be breaking the first and most important of my Middle School Survival Rules. Rule Number One: *Never speak to anyone except adults, and then only if they ask you a direct question.* The Rules could never be broken, no matter what.

I heard a snort and a breathy laugh, and then Madison's heels clicked away down the aisle. A comment followed them just loud enough for me and the adoring crowd in the back seats.

"Did you see the fish eyes on Trash Licker Junior?" The back-seat crowd let loose with a laugh particular to middle schoolers, the kind that could strip the paint from concrete.

Antonia shook my elbow. "Why is everybody laughing?" she asked. "Who's Trash Licker Junior?"

I didn't answer her, even when she started pinching my arm. My eyes had closed. It wasn't perfectly black behind my lids because of the dancing sunspots, but it would do. If I couldn't see the world, then the world couldn't see me either.

I knew it was stupid and childish. But for a few moments, I pretended I was all alone in the world—no other kids, no school, and especially no Antonia. It didn't matter if in about fifteen minutes I'd have to open my eyes again with the whole rotten year ahead of me. For fifteen minutes, I could pretend none of that mattered.

So while Antonia poked and prodded at me, asking me to explain what was so funny, I shut down and disappeared. That's what I did best.

4

"**LOOK AT ALL** this," Antonia said, gawking at the cafeteria like it was the Grand Canyon. Her pink kitten backpack was still overloaded and slung pointlessly on her shoulder. I wondered if she'd taken it off since the morning. Her eyes darted in every direction, and she swiveled her head back and forth like an automatic sprinkler. "This is way bigger than my old school."

Somehow, I'd managed to get through the morning classes without anyone really noticing or caring I was there. I'd snagged Antonia as she spilled out of her reading intensive and dragged her to the cafeteria before too much of a line formed. Only seven kids in front of us. I closed my eyes and breathed.

4576, 4576, 4576, I kept repeating in my head. My lunch ID number, the one I'd need to punch into the keypad to pay for my meal, was the same one I'd had last year. But I wasn't taking any chances.

"Do we have an assigned table? Can we sit where we want? Do they have pepperoni pizza?" The questions tumbled out faster than I could handle. Not that I tried to give Antonia any answers. I just grabbed a tray for her and one for myself and slid mine along the metal bars.

Now only four stood in line ahead of us. A damp hamburger and a dish of slightly green tater tots cowered miserably on my tray. The smell of floor cleaner and grease left over from 1964 combined into some unnatural fumes. More than likely it caused brain damage, which would explain a lot about middle school.

Antonia was still jabbering away about something or other. I figured if I at least got us to the lunch table, she could jabber on all she wanted. I'd make an excuse later about why no one sat with us, why my eyes stayed locked on my tray and never looked up except to check the slowest clock in the world, and why I never said a word to anyone.

4576, 4576, take one hamburger, one dish of tater tots, one dish of peas, one milk, one fork, one napkin, punch in the number, walk to the round table, sit, eat, wait, 4576, 4576—

I had the drill down cold. In five minutes, we'd sit down. After thirty-seven more, lunch would finally be over— sometimes eaten, sometimes not. I usually felt less queasy when it wasn't. Ninety-four minutes after that, the school day would end. Twenty-five minutes later, we'd hear the whoosh of the bus doors close behind us. And sixteen hours later, the whole ordeal would start all over again.

Whoopee.

4576, 4576, 4576—

Antonia tugged at my sleeve. "Lucy, Lucy, Lucy," she chanted in her much-too-loud voice, "which one's our table, huh? Tell me! Where do you and your friends sit?"

"Friends?" a familiar voice said from farther down the lunch line. "What friends?"

No, no, no, please no. I didn't have to turn around to recognize Madison's snarl. The snorting noises that followed every nasty word she spat out had to be Ashley and Gretta. I tried not to listen, but the words still found me and drilled right into my brain.

"Who'd want to be friends with Trash Licker? She smells like cat puke."

"Oh, Maddie! You're so mean!"

"Soooo mean!"

I peeked a glance at Antonia to see how she was taking this, but she was oblivious. Fine by me. The icy fingers, though, were squeezing the breath out of my lungs.

4576, 4576, 4576, please, please—

"It's true. Even bug-eyed Trash Licker Junior smells like it. That's because cat puke's all they can find at the dump."

"The dump? Gross!"

"Ew!"

Shut up, shut up, 4576, 4576, 4576—

Only one person ahead of us. All I had to do was punch in the lunch code and I'd be set. Madison and her followers always clustered near the long row of windows, far, far away from my table. She could trash-talk me all she wanted from there. We wouldn't hear a word of it. Even so, the icy fingers squeezed harder and harder with every breath I sucked in.

4576, 4576, 4576—

"They go there every night for dinner. Eating cat puke and rat heads."

"No! Gross! You don't mean for real. Is that for real?"

"Ew!"

Finally, I reached the register. A sharp pain stabbed between my eyes. Everything was blurry. My shaking fingers paused before the keypad.

Okay, okay, 4756, 4756 . . .

My heart skipped a beat. *Wait. Were those the right numbers? Is it 456—no, 47—no, what is it—what is it—*

"Put them in already." The lunch lady at the cash register, new to me, wore too much makeup and looked bored. MRS. DUDLEY was scrawled on her name tag in Magic Marker.

My fingers couldn't stop shaking. Those four numbers, the same ones I'd been punching in day after day for a whole year, had suddenly dissolved.

"Put them in already," Madison mocked in a high voice. The twins snickered.

"You want me to do it?" Antonia asked. She reached over and banged keypad buttons at random.

"Stop that," Mrs. Dudley snapped. She grabbed Antonia by the wrist and swung it away. "You're holding up the line.

If you don't know your credit code, lunch is three dollars and forty-five cents."

"Nuh-uh," Antonia said, blowing on her wrist. "Not for us. We don't have to pay anything. We get our lunch for free."

Mrs. Dudley raised her eyebrows. Laughter ran down the line. And the icy fingers reached up and grabbed me by the throat.

We'd been on the free lunch program since arriving at Oneega Valley because Mom's pay was so low. So were a quarter of the kids in the school. But no one bragged about it. No one ever talked about it. Because if you let a certain kind of person know you're poor, they can turn mean. Ugly mean.

"Hear that?" Mrs. Dudley said over her shoulder in a very loud voice. "She gets her lunch for *free*."

Two beady eyes and a hairnet appeared in a small window behind Mrs. Dudley. They disappeared for a moment, then popped back into view.

"She's 4576," a husky voice growled from the back. "And her sister's 3827." I banged the numbers in frantically one after the other and took my tray from the lunch line. I hoped Antonia was following me, but I didn't dare look.

"Think they don't have to pay for nothing," Mrs. Dudley grumbled as I slunk away. "Maybe somebody at home should try working for a change."

My hands shook even after I sat down at the round table. Antonia, who thankfully had followed after all, set down her tray next to me. She didn't sit, though. She remained standing with her head tilted to one side, staring back at the lunch line.

"Why'd that lady say that?" she asked.

"Sit down," I whispered.

"But why'd she say that?"

"Please sit down," I whispered again, as loud as I dared. Antonia finally sat, but her eyes never left the lunch line.

"Mom works," she said.

I nudged the pile of the green-tinged tater tots around with a plastic spoon. "I know," I said quietly. "Eat your lunch."

"Works hard every day." Antonia faced me. Her cheeks were colored a blotchy pink. "She don't know nothing about Mom."

I squeezed my eyes shut and gritted my teeth. "Please," I begged her. "Let it go."

Antonia scowled. Then she took off her backpack, propped it in her lap, and buried her face in it. I could hear her mumbling something, but I wasn't going to make a scene about it.

Of all the different ways I'd played out this day's lunchtime in my head, I'd never planned for this. Why did I let Madison get to me like that? She didn't say anything she hadn't said a hundred times before, and worse. And why couldn't Antonia keep her big mouth shut? Mom was always going on about how I should be more patient with her because she couldn't help the way she was. Sometimes I wondered if Antonia didn't take advantage of her "helplessness" more than Mom realized.

None of that mattered now. I didn't look up, but I could feel dozens and dozens of eyes zeroed in on us—the stupid girl who wouldn't talk to anyone and her crazy, loudmouth sister who was moaning into her baby backpack. A couple of pathetic losers.

Trash Licker and Trash Licker Junior.

My eyes started to burn. *Please don't cry please don't cry,* I pleaded silently, even as the sobs rose up my throat.

Then the table suddenly jerked and banged into my ribs. I swallowed the sob and opened my eyes, ready to glare at Antonia for her clumsiness, which was about all I could do. What I didn't expect was the sight of the big, goofy grin plastered all over my sister's face.

"This is going to be good," she said.

Antonia shoved aside her lunch tray, planted her backpack on the table with a thud, and rested her chin on it, all the while still grinning like a cat with a mouse under each paw. Now I was really worried. She must have snapped under the pressure and lost her mind. I couldn't blame her. It was a miracle the same thing hadn't happened to me a long time ago.

"Antonia—" I started, but she held up her hand.

"Watch," she said. "You'll see."

You'll see? A vision of Antonia bolting out of her chair to tackle Mrs. Dudley and shove carrot sticks up the lunch lady's nose wandered through my brain. Part of me dreaded it. Another part of me wondered how far she could jam them up there before someone pulled her off.

But Antonia didn't move. She just sat there grinning her big, dumb grin and drumming her fingers.

What on earth does she think's going to happen? I pretended not to care, deciding that lining up my shriveled peas in groups of three was the most useful thing I could do. *Let her sit there and grin all she wants. Nothing's going to happen.*

And for the second time that day, I was dead wrong.

I heard it before I saw it—like the rumble of a distant train. A strange clattering rang out from the lunch line. I turned to see what the commotion was.

Mrs. Dudley stood by the large aluminum basket holding the half pints of milk and chocolate milk. Her face was pinched with confusion.

No wonder. The milk basket was rattling and shaking and bouncing from side to side, the cartons flipping and knocking into each other.

Nobody was touching it.

Mrs. Dudley reached out a finger to touch the basket. It clanged loudly. She drew her finger back quickly, like she'd been given a shock.

"Emma? Something's wrong with the milk," Mrs. Dudley said, trying to sound calm and not succeeding very well.

"I already checked the expiration dates," the husky voice called out from the back.

"No, I don't mean the milk's gone bad," Mrs. Dudley said. "It's—it's *moving*."

"What?"

"I said—"

Bang!

The aluminum basket jumped up out of its metal slot about a foot, hovered for a second, then slammed back down. Mrs. Dudley shrieked. By this time every head in the lunchroom had turned to watch. No one said a word. No one moved.

The basket leaped up a second time. Mrs. Dudley grabbed it on both sides and tried to shove it back down. The milk basket didn't budge from its place in midair.

"Stop it! Stop it!" she yelled. It slammed down a second time, then started bouncing up and down more rapidly, going a little bit higher each time. Mrs. Dudley's face changed from pasty fear to tomato-red rage. She kept her hand clamped tight to the basket, even when it leaped so high she was barely standing on her tiptoes, bellowing out words not exactly school appropriate.

Antonia punched me lightly on the arm. "Here we go," she said.

Before I could ask what she meant, the basket dropped down and the banging stopped. The room went completely quiet except for Mrs. Dudley's heavy breathing. She hunched over the basket with her hands gripping the sides. Thick veins stuck out in her neck, and a satisfied look of victory spread across her red, sweaty face.

"Got you," she wheezed.

And that's when the milk exploded.

Every carton burst open at the top and shot its contents straight into Mrs. Dudley's startled face like wet fireworks. The volley of milk hit her so hard she was thrown a foot in the air. She rode the brown-and-white wave for a moment until gravity took over, and she fell back on her bottom with a huge, damp plop.

Even after she landed, a downpour of white and chocolate milk continued to rain on her. She didn't move or try to get out of the way. She just sat there blinking with her mouth open, adrift in a huge, swirly lake of milk. Finally, the last of it sputtered out of the ruined cartons.

For about five seconds, there was complete silence, except for the *drip drip* of milk from her hairnet and the click of the minute hand on the wall clock.

Then Mrs. Dudley screamed.

After that, it was chaos. Kids doubled up with laughter while adults burst into the lunchroom and ran in every direction, shouting and pointing fingers and sometimes slipping in the milky puddles pooled up and down the lunch line.

It was the strangest thing I'd ever seen. But what was even stranger was how Antonia sat there the whole time clutching her backpack to her stomach, rocking back and forth, smiling like she'd never stop smiling the rest of her life.

5

WATCH, YOU'LL SEE. That's what Antonia had said right before the milk exploded. And then there was that big grin she'd had stuck on her face after the whole show. At first I wondered if she'd had something to do with it. But that made no sense. I mean, how could a girl who wore a baby-duck barrette pull off such a stunt?

The answer came easily—she hadn't done anything. It was only a coincidence.

It was just like Antonia to take credit for a coincidence. Once, when she was seven, she dreamed it would rain. Later that day, despite the weatherman's predictions, it drizzled a little. For a long time after, she insisted she'd made it happen and she was a dream wizard, even though she could never make any of her other dreams come true since.

This was the same thing. A coincidence—a very weird coincidence, sure, but still a coincidence.

The cafeteria incident was all anyone in the school talked

about the rest of the afternoon. The "Atomic Milk Bomb" and "Revenge of the Cows" were a few of the names I overheard. The teachers were the worst. After shushing the kids and scolding them for gossiping, they'd whisper to each other and hide their smirks behind closed fists like they were coughing.

No one bothered with me. The Milk Bomb made me invisible. Even Madison didn't evil-eye me when she walked into Ms. Crozzetti's social studies class—the only class we shared, thankfully. She was too busy chattering with the twins. As first days went, this one hadn't turned out half bad. And heading to Mr. Capp's art class at the end of it was the whipped-cream frosting on the stale and just-barely-edible first-day-of-school cupcake.

I'd knew I'd be okay once I got to Mr. Capp's class. He was the best, and I loved knowing he was going to be my art teacher again.

He never asked me any embarrassing questions, and he always had little tasks for me to do, like cleaning brushes or sorting colored beads. And about once a week he had me draw a dog.

The dog thing started the year before in November, just before the Thanksgiving break. We were supposed to be constructing a color wheel. Usually I do what I'm told, but that day I was copying the little beagle from the cover of *Shiloh* onto the back of my notebook. I'd borrowed the book that morning from the library, mostly because of the cover. I love any book about animals, and I'd read *Black Beauty* about a thousand times, but something about that dog's face just warmed my heart.

Daddy used to talk about getting a dog, but talk was all he ever did about it, which was pretty typical for him. The trailer park we lived in now didn't allow pets, but that didn't keep me from daydreaming about a cute pup to cuddle. So that day, without thinking, I picked up my pencil and started drawing.

My face burned once I realized Mr. Capp was watching me. Last year I hadn't known him very well, or how nice he could be. I was so scared I didn't even try to hide what I was doing.

I waited for the red-faced screaming and the detention slip I probably had coming. After a minute of silence, I braved a quick glance up. His forehead was all knotted like he was thinking hard. He didn't look mad, but I could never tell with adults.

"Not bad." He crooked his finger and directed me to sit at the table by the window. I did as I was told, even though my legs felt like cement. He disappeared in his art closet for a few seconds, then came out with a huge book the size of a mailbox. He slammed the book on the table, opened it up, and pointed to a picture of a beagle.

"Try and draw that for me," he said, and walked away.

For five minutes, I sat there trembling, my pencil frozen in my fingers, not moving a muscle. Was this a trick? Some kind of weird adult game to trap me? My daddy used to be like that. Smiling one minute like he was everybody's best friend and then, without warning, throwing out angry words like knives, not caring much who he cut.

After a very long and very painful five minutes, I finally lifted my eyes. Mr. Capp was leaning back in his chair with his feet propped on his desk. He was gazing out the window and tapping a pencil on his chin. And then he stopped, turned to me, and smiled.

He smiled at me for all of two seconds, then went back to tapping his chin. And that was it. But something in me kind of unwound a little. I can't explain why. And I started drawing.

Since that time I'd said maybe six words to him. He still talked to me every class, though, like we were having a regular conversation. I must have drawn at least a couple dozen different dogs for him. Once in a while one of them would show up somewhere on a wall or a bulletin board. And for a little while that day I'd float a couple of inches above the ground.

So for forty-two minutes, twice a week, I could unclench my stomach and relax. I was safe with Mr. Capp. That was a pretty big deal.

Some kids made fun of Mr. Capp behind his back. He'd married the guy he'd lived with for twenty years once it became legal in New York. Their picture was in the paper, smiling and holding hands. I thought they looked sweet together.

Happy. I hoped I could feel happy like that when I was an adult.

But I did feel *almost* happy when I entered his class that afternoon after all the lunchtime craziness. And almost happy was good enough.

"There you are, Lucy," Mr. Capp said as I walked in. Like always, he wore a pale blue painter's smock, and the ends of his big black mustache were twisted so they pointed up like a bug's antennae. He held a large cardboard box in both hands.

"Come here and give me a hand," he said. "I need you to sort through these colored pencils and pull out all the broken ones." He leaned in closer and lowered his voice. "I hope you don't mind, but I'm making you table partners with a girl who's new to the school. Her name is May Darasavath. Her family moved here from the city about a week ago, so she's probably feeling a little out of sorts. You don't have to do anything special with her but be your usual wonderful self. That work for you, Lucy?"

I looked at the girl sitting at the front table. She had a long waterfall of black hair and friendly brown eyes. "Sure," I said, and I brought the tub of pencils over to the table.

I found out pretty quickly that for a girl who, according to Mr. Capp, was "feeling a little out of sorts," she sure didn't hold back. While we both sorted the pencils, she talked to me about her little brother, who had a head like a pumpkin and who ate his boogers; about her left pinkie toe, which was abnormally larger than all her other toes but was still her favorite; about the best television show ever, called *Demon Donnie*, about a half-human, half-demon teenage boy who had a good heart and awesome hair and couldn't help it if everything he touched blew up; and about a thousand other things all jumbled up together in words that spilled constantly out of her mouth.

Once in a while she'd turn to me and say, "What do you think?" And I'd nod or mumble, "Uh, yeah . . . great," or something just as meaningless. Sometimes I even smiled. But she didn't seem to mind keeping up the conversation for both of us. And the funny thing is, neither did I. I liked May right away, and strangely enough, I think she may have liked me. Or at least she didn't hate me, which was okay too. *Whipped-cream frosting with a cherry on top*, I thought.

By the time I stepped onto the bus after the last bell, I'd half convinced myself this year might not be as horrible as I'd imagined. After all, the honors for having the worst first day ever had to go to the lunch lady. And to be honest, I didn't feel too bad about what happened to Mrs. Dudley. Antonia was right. That woman shouldn't have talked about Mom that way.

I worried about Antonia, though. She didn't say much sitting next to me on the bus and kept her head buried in her backpack like she'd done at lunchtime. I wondered if her cafeteria grin was only an act, her way of pretending she wasn't bothered by Mrs. Dudley's nastiness. Or maybe she'd really convinced herself she'd made the Milk Bomb happen, and now she was feeling guilty about hurting some-one.

I touched the back of her hand. She turned it over and wrapped her fingers in mine. We stayed like that the whole way home.

I thought about raiding my coffee-can bank for the Christmas half-dollars I'd been saving. A couple of fat choc-olate bars from the convenience store would be just the thing to perk up my sister. Especially if they had almonds.

The bus slowed and let us off. As it pulled away, I tapped Antonia on the shoulder to share my candy bar idea. Before I could get out a word, she grabbed hold of my sleeve.

"Come on!" she said, yanking me behind her as she rushed on ahead. She was smaller than me, but her grip was a steel vise, and I stumbled along as best as I could. When we got to the ginkgo tree, she pushed me hard onto the stony ground.

"Ouch," I said, rubbing my bottom. "Watch what you're doing."

Antonia didn't hear a word I said. She danced around the tree, flailing her arms, kicking up her feet, and letting loose with several earsplitting howler-monkey screams.

"What's gotten into you?" I yelled.

Antonia ignored me. She stopped to watch the bus as it turned the corner. When it disappeared completely, she stuck out her tongue and blew a wet raspberry. Then she plopped herself right next to me.

"So . . . what did you think?" Antonia was grinning like she had at the lunch table. It was starting to get on my nerves.

"About what?" I asked. "Like how you almost broke my butt bone?"

Antonia groaned and rolled her eyes. "Not that! You know. *Spoosh!*" She puckered her lips and wiggled her fingers in the air.

"Oh, the milk," I said, still rubbing. "Yeah, I guess that was kind of weird."

"Did you see her face?"

"The lunch lady? Sure. She was pretty upset."

Antonia snorted. "Serves her right." She pulled her backpack to her lap, zipped it open, and stuck her face deep inside. At first I thought she was searching for something. But then I heard her whispering.

"Antonia?" I said.

She laughed and lifted her head. "It was all her idea, you know. About the milk. Wasn't that a good idea?"

"What are you talking about?" I asked. "Whose idea?"

"Whose? *Hers.*" Her hand dove into her backpack. Sheets of paper, notebooks, and gnawed pencils were flung carelessly over her shoulder. Then she jammed her tongue in the corner of her mouth and strained at whatever was stuck in the bottom of her bag.

Finally, with a loud grunt, her arm jerked free. More paper and pencils shot in all directions, followed by a huge yellow cloud that swallowed both her hands. Antonia kicked the backpack aside and smoothed the cloud in her lap until it settled into loose blond curls. Then she spun it around to face me.

The doll's head. She was holding the doll's head.

6

MY STOMACH FLUTTERED like it did on stormy nights, when the tree branches rattled like dead bones. Maybe it was the dark space in the eye socket where Antonia had cleaned out the mud, or the tiny smirk on the doll's thin lips I hadn't noticed before. Or it might have been the thought of Antonia with a battered doll's head buried in her backpack at school all day long. *Ugh.*

I frowned. "Why did you bring that to school?"

"I told her what that lunch lady said," Antonia said, ignoring my question. "She thought it was mean. She said mean people like that need to know what it feels like to be treated like garbage." Her bottom lip trembled a little. "Mom's not garbage."

"I know," I said. "Mrs. Dudley shouldn't have said those things. But why did you bring that—that *thing* to school?"

Antonia covered the doll's ears with her hands and glared at me. "She is not a thing," she whispered. "She has a name.

Hush-a-bye. Like in that song Mom sings when it storms and the thunder hurts my ears. I sang it to her last night." She closed her eyes and warbled a little off-key.

> *Hush-a-bye and good night*
> *Till the bright morning light*
> *Takes the sleep from your eyes*
> *Hush-a-bye, baby bright*

"Fine." I gritted my teeth and resisted the urge to do something hurtful. "Why did you bring *Hush-a-bye* to school? Don't you know what kids would say if they saw you brought a doll's head to school?"

Antonia uncovered Hush-a-bye's ears. She tilted the head toward her and smiled. "They'd say, 'Hello, pretty girl with the curly blond hair.'"

The urge won out. I threw a twig at Antonia and hit her smack between the eyes. "No," I said as she scowled at me. "They'd call you a weirdo. Is that how you want to start middle school? As the class weirdo? How do you expect to make any friends when everyone's making fun of you?"

Antonia's chin sank down to her chest, and she sucked in her lips. Her pouty face. I didn't care. She had to hear the truth whether she liked it or not, for her own good. *If I were an only child, I wouldn't have to put up with Antonia's nonsense.* The idea flashed in my brain briefly, but I let it go. This wasn't the time for mean thoughts.

"I don't want to make you feel bad," I said, trying to sound a little less harsh, "but if you're going to make any friends this year—"

"Hush-a-bye asked me a question on the bus," Antonia interrupted. "She was wondering where *your* friends were at lunch today."

The question stopped me cold. Antonia's head was still down, but the doll's single green eye was looking straight at me like she already knew the answer.

"I don't know what you mean," I said.

"All the other kids sat with their friends." Antonia raised her eyes to mine. "How come you didn't?"

I waved my hands in circles like it was no big deal. Really I was stalling until I could think up a good excuse. "Oh. That. It was . . . You know . . . I . . . I wanted it to be just you and me for lunch and . . . and wasn't that milk explosion the weirdest thing?"

Antonia's face brightened. "The milk!" she howled, and doubled over with laughter. "That was a good one."

"Must have been some kind of freak accident," I said, relieved Antonia had stopped asking me any more questions about my nonexistent friends.

Antonia shook her head vigorously. "No, no, no. That was Hush-a-bye. She *made* it happen."

"She made it happen," I repeated. It wasn't the craziest story Antonia had ever made up. When she was eight, she'd insisted a swarm of wasp angels lived under her pillow and had made her their supreme queen.

Except she wasn't eight anymore. This wasn't a good sign. Maybe she'd had a hard first day in middle school, and this was her way of running from it. Running from problems was something I knew a lot about.

Part of me wanted to help her, tell her she didn't need to make up stories. I'd be there for her—and I'd stop imagining what it would be like if she didn't exist. I'd be her big, strong older sister who'd protect her from all the middle school crud that might crawl under her skin and slowly worm its way into her heart.

But another part of me knew that would never happen, not in a million years, and wanted desperately to avoid any more questions I didn't want to answer. I knew which part would win out.

"How did she manage that?" I asked.

Antonia scratched her head. "I don't understand it all exactly. It's kind of like magic, except I have to want it real bad to make it happen. Real bad. She can't just do it because she feels like it. So I asked and I asked and then she could do it. The asking is like a key that opens up her magic."

"A key?"

Antonia nodded. "Yeah. A key that opens up a door of magic somewhere in her heart and lets it come outside. But some other kind of magic goes back inside her too and fills *her* up. That's the best part! She gets some magic back to herself, a good kind of magic that helps her. That's why I took you to this tree. She said something special was waiting here."

Antonia sat Hush-a-bye against the ginkgo trunk. She snaked her fingers through the dry grass around the tree's base, searching for the special whatever, her face pinched in concentration. I stood and looked vaguely around, not having a clue what I was supposed to find.

Then Antonia gasped and she pounced on a spot in the grass.

"Oh! Oh!" she squealed, holding up a fist with yellow grass blades poking through. "It's true! It's true!"

I squinted at her balled-up fingers, trying to figure out what she'd found. Whatever it was, it couldn't be very big.

Antonia opened her hand and picked out the bits of grass. She licked her thumb and rubbed at the thing in her palm. Her eyes grew big.

"Oh, Hush-a-bye," she whispered. "It's beautiful."

I craned my neck to see. "What have you got? Better not be a bug."

She snatched Hush-a-bye from the trunk without answering, then sat hunched over the doll with her back to me. I was a little miffed at being kept in the dark. I wasn't used to Antonia keeping secrets from me.

"I'm not going to sit here all day and wait for you," I said, a little snippily.

"All done," Antonia said. "Come and see."

I thought about dragging my feet so Antonia would know I wasn't happy waiting, but my curiosity got the better of me. I ran around to face her.

Antonia sat cross-legged with Hush-a-bye in her lap. Her face shone with sweat, and her eyes gleamed.

"Look." She turned Hush-a-bye's head so I could see the doll's face.

At first it looked like the same busted-up doll's head I'd pulled out of the riverbank, only a little cleaner. Hush-a-bye's head rocked back and forth in Antonia's fingers, and the afternoon light flashed off the doll's eyes.

A strange thought crawled through my brain. *It's laughing at me.* Then a shiver went up my spine.

I'd heard that expression before, but I'd never really understood what it meant until then—like someone sliding a cold, dead finger up the middle of your back. But I didn't shiver because of some imaginary laugh I didn't hear. I shivered at what I saw.

The empty space in Hush-a-bye's left socket was now filled with a brand-new, bright green eye.

7

THE NEXT DAY, I convinced Antonia to not bring Hush-a-bye to school in her backpack anymore. I told her someone might steal the doll if they knew it could do magic. This put Antonia into an immediate panic. Before she left for school, she stuck Hush-a-bye in a plastic bag and stuffed it in the back of her underwear drawer.

By that time, I'd decided Hush-a-bye's new eye was something Antonia had found near the river. She must have stuffed it in her pocket, maybe one with a hole, and after it fell out, she forgot she'd ever had it in the first place. Why she'd want a single doll's eye, I couldn't figure out, but there was a lot of things Antonia did that didn't make sense. Like bringing a busted doll's head to school.

As for the Milk Bomb, the word around school was that spoiled milk was to blame for what happened in the cafeteria. Some kind of nasty bacteria gas must have bubbled up in the cartons until they finally blew up, which also explained why the milk basket jumped. It seemed as good a reason as any.

After taking two "personal" days off, Mrs. Dudley, the lunch lady, showed up for work. She pretended like nothing happened, but every time someone rattled the milk basket, she'd flinch. It got rattled a *lot*. It didn't surprise me. I knew as well as anyone you could always count on a certain group of kids to kick someone when they're down. Then again, if anyone deserved a good kick, it was Mrs. Dudley.

After a week and a half, the big event faded, and life at the middle school went back to normal. Which wasn't the best thing in the world.

I managed as best as I could. The days came and went, some tolerable, some less so. Mr. Capp's class was still a forty-two-minute-long bright spot, and listening to May Darasavath chatter away about nothing in particular made it shine a little brighter.

The worst part of the day was the three minutes between social studies and science class. Three minutes. One hundred and eighty seconds. Doesn't sound like much, but it was the longest three minutes of my day.

Every day, after social studies ended, Madison would walk close behind me, an Oslo twin flanking her on each side. And every day she'd beat me down to a pulp.

I don't mean she actually hit me. Madison never poked me or pinched me or tripped me or slammed me up against the lockers. She never laid a single manicured fingernail on my scrawny body. Her weapon was whispers. She never did it in front of any adults who could call her out, and none of the kids cared enough about me to stop her.

"Did you see that?" she'd start once we left the social studies classroom.

"What? What?" one of the twins would answer.

"A couple of cockroaches crawled out of Trash Licker's hair and down her shirt."

"No. Really? Gross!"

"Really. Probably her pets."

"Ew! You're so bad, Maddie!"

Worse was when Madison talked about my parents—that is, the people she pretended were my parents.

"You know what I heard," Madison would say, "I heard her daddy's on death row. I can't even tell you what he did, it's so awful. And I saw her mom picking through the garbage bins at the supermarket, looking for their dinner. She has a face like a weasel, and her teeth are brown and rotten. It's no wonder Trash Licker's the way she is."

I wished I could have swung around and screamed at her, or smashed my fist right into her perfect white teeth, or told everyone who was listening some awful thing about Madison that would make her cry and run away. But I never did. Not even close.

Against the Rules, you know—specifically Rule Number Four.

Madison didn't know about the Middle School Survival

Rules. No one did except for the person who'd invented them, and the person who was under very strict orders to follow them without question. Both of them were me.

The Rules took effect from the moment I stepped onto the bus in the morning until its taillights disappeared around the corner in the afternoon. They weren't written down anywhere, but I stuck by them every single day without fail.

1. Never speak to anyone except adults, and then only if they ask you a direct question.

2. When moving from one class to another, keep your books tight to your chest, your head down, and move as quickly as possible without touching anyone.

3. Get to the cafeteria before it gets crowded to grab the small round table. If you're too late, hide in the bathroom until lunch is over.

4. When other kids talk about you and call you terrible names, do nothing. When they trip you and knock the books out of your hand and elbow you in the stomach, do nothing. When you don't know what else to do, do nothing.

5. If you feel like crying, dig your nails into your

palms. Then when you're at home, take a pillow into the bathroom and bury your face in it until the tears stop and remind yourself that school won't last forever, even if most of the time it feels like it'll never end.

The idea of the Middle School Survival Rules started last year, on my first day of sixth grade here in Oneega Valley. I'd just moved to the town two days before, at the tail end of September. We were still living in the local shelter, but Mom insisted on signing us up for school as quickly as possible.

I was shuffled into Mrs. Wilbur's homeroom class on a Tuesday morning wearing my last clean T-shirt tucked into a pair of raggedy jeans with a hole in one pocket and two broken belt loops. Eighteen pairs of eyes stared at me like I was some wild dog who'd wandered into the class. I decided to study the toes of my dirty sneakers with fierce concentration.

Mrs. Wilbur had pressed her bony hand on my shoulder. "Listen up, class," she'd said. "This is Lucy Bloom. She's just moved here from Chat-a . . . Chau-ter . . . from another county. Let's make sure we all—Billy, take that pencil out of your nose right now! Let's make her feel welcome in our classroom. So, Lucy, why don't you tell us a little about yourself?"

I'd squinted up at the roomful of gawking eyes, and I opened my mouth. Nothing came out.

Tell a little about myself? What could I tell? How Mom had snuck us out of our house at midnight while Daddy, full out of his mind with whiskey, shot out the windows with his Glock? How we left Chautauqua County with Antonia snoring in the back seat while Mom drove with one white-knuckled hand on the wheel with the other hand pressed a bag of melting ice against her swollen cheek? Or how we ended up in Oneega Valley because it's where our car finally ran out of gas, or what it was like living on cots in a damp shelter eating nothing but crackers and baked beans because they were the only groceries donated that week, or how Mom sobbed into her pillow every night when she thought I was asleep?

I didn't want anyone to know anything about me. I just wanted to melt through the floorboards and never be seen again.

Instead, my mouth stayed open, as if the muscles in my jaw had locked. The other sixth graders kept staring at me. Mrs. Wilbur wrinkled her forehead, slowly realizing this may not have been the best idea. All I did was stand there like a lump of uselessness. Nothing came out of my mouth. Nothing would either, not if she'd kept me there for a hundred years.

At least, that's what I thought at the time. But once again, I was wrong.

I'd leaned forward a little, my mouth still gaping open. The girl sitting in the front row leaned in toward me like she wanted to hear better. She wore a bright red top, and she had the most beautiful brown eyes I'd ever seen. I wanted to tell her that.

Instead, I threw up all over her desk. I guess something did come out after all.

Everything after that's still kind of a blur. Maybe I don't want to remember. I don't know. All I do know is not too many people asked me questions after that. Which was fine by me.

But I did learn that girl's name. Madison Underwood. Maddie to her friends. She made it clear pretty quickly I wouldn't ever be one of those. Not after what I did to her. And with a little whispering here and there, no one else would either.

And that's exactly what happened. I became the friendless Trash Licker. And all the nasty laughter and disgusted stares and mean jokes piled on top of me and slowly crushed me like a cockroach. But just like a roach, I kept scurrying along.

I never told anyone what was going on at school—not the school psychologist, who knew how we ended up in Oneega Valley and told me her door was always open; not my favorite teacher, Mr. Capp; or my sister, Antonia; or even Mom. I didn't say a single word.

It's not like I didn't know what I was supposed to do—ignore the bullying, stand up for myself, or tell a friend or an adult. Part of me really did want to tell someone. Anyone.

But I didn't do that. Maybe it was because my brain was already a pile of mush from all the terrible things we'd already gone through with Daddy. I don't know.

But the longer it went on, the harder it got to say anything. I'd convinced myself I waited too long, and I was afraid no one would believe me, or maybe they'd start hating me too. So instead of asking for help, I came up with the Rules. I followed them every day without fail. I had to. I didn't know what else to do.

"HOW'S MIDDLE SCHOOL going for my firecrackers?"
Mom said, slapping margarine on a piece of white bread like
she wanted to show it who was boss.

Mom insisted we have regular sit-down family meals every Friday no matter what. She said the twelve-hour shifts
she had to work every Saturday and Sunday left her a pile of
goo on the weekend, so this was her only chance to catch up
with her girls. I never understood why she claimed dinner-
time was so important since she spent most of it reminding
Antonia to keep her elbows off the table and stop picking her
teeth with her thumbnail.

"My locker gets jammed all the time and I have to kick
it," Antonia said as she stuck beans on the end of her fork
with her fingers. "Today I was almost late for music. But
guess what? Gus Albero did some kind of a trick with it. He
whacked it hard in the middle and opened it right up."

"You're lucky he didn't break it," I said.

Antonia gave me the stink eye. "He wasn't going to break it. He was helping me." She smirked. "He likes me."

Mom's butter knife paused in midair. "What makes you think he likes you?"

"He asked me if I was going to the Halloween dance."

Both of Mom's eyebrows shot up, which meant she was surprised. If only one went up, that meant trouble. "He asked you to a dance?"

"Not exactly." Antonia pulled off one bean and rolled it between her finger and thumb. "He asked me if I was thinking of going."

"What did you say?" I asked.

"I said I was thinking about it." Antonia squashed her bean and popped it into her mouth. "I was thinking me and Lucy could go together. She and me and Gus and whoever she wanted to bring."

Before I could raise a fuss about that impossible situation, Mom gave a little wave with her knife. "Antonia Willa Bloom, you need to cool your jets. I don't recall anyone asking me for permission." She held up her hand before Antonia could start begging. "That's still six weeks away. I'm not going to talk about it now. How about we see how you do on your five-week progress report first, hm?"

Antonia grumbled a little, but she didn't argue. At least she knew better than to pick a fight with Mom right then and ruin her chance to go completely. That meant I didn't have to think about it for a while either, which was fine by me. Unlike Mom, I wasn't surprised someone asked her to the dance. Despite the duckling barrette, Antonia was a pretty girl. It was just a matter of time before some boy noticed. I just wished it was someone better than Gus.

The rest of dinner went quiet, except for Antonia's openmouthed chewing. She finished first, like always, and scooted to our room. I followed after helping Mom with the dishes.

When I opened our bedroom door, the room was empty. "Antonia?"

After I closed the door behind me, I heard murmuring drifting over from the closet. Was Antonia talking to the doll in there again? She'd spoken to it behind the closet door every day since we found it, which was strange even for her. I could never hear what she was saying, though, and I got curious. What do you talk about to a broken doll's head anyway?

I snuck up closer and pressed my ear against the closet door. The murmuring stopped.

"Antonia?" I said.

The door slid open. Antonia was wedged in the little chair with Hush-a-bye set in front of her and stuck back on the cardboard box.

The head looked different somehow. Not just the new eye. Her face had fewer scratches than before, and her chipped-up nose was more filled in. Even her blond hair seemed thicker and curlier. I figured Antonia must have been working hard to spruce her up, but something about the changes still unsettled me.

"What are you doing?" I asked.

Antonia shrugged. "Just talking to Hush-a-bye. Why?"

"No reason." *Whatever.* I jerked my chin at Hush-a-bye. "How does she like living in the closet?"

"She's tired of being stuck on a box," Antonia said. "Tomorrow we're going to look for her body."

I laughed. "Her body probably floated out to the ocean and was eaten by a tiger shark. Are you going shark-hunting?"

Antonia glared at me. "Wait and see. You won't be laughing tomorrow." She slammed the closet door closed. The murmuring started up again.

I stood there staring at the door. Antonia could be so touchy sometimes. I had half a mind to open the closet, grab the doll's head, and toss it in the trash can behind our trailer. Instead, I pressed my ear against the door again and listened.

Antonia's voice was muffled. I put my finger in my other ear to hear better, but it didn't help. Then my knee bumped against the door.

Antonia's voice stopped. I didn't want Antonia to think I was spying on her, so I didn't move a muscle.

A few seconds passed. Still nothing but silence. My knees started to cramp, so I decided to give up and shuffle away as quiet as possible. I moved one foot back, and a thick whisper came through the door.

"Good night, Lucy, sleep tight."

I backed away from the door, no longer trying to be careful, and banged into the side of Antonia's bed. I crawled over it into my own bed and burrowed under my covers.

As I lay there, I thought about the whisper I'd heard and played it back over and over in my head.

Good night, Lucy, sleep tight.

It was an oven under all those blankets, but I couldn't stop shaking. The whisper from the closet was garbled and thick, like someone trying to talk through a mouthful of mud.

But more than that, the voice I'd heard wasn't Antonia's.

I'D BARELY WOKEN up when Antonia pulled my leg so hard I slipped from under my covers and fell on the floor.

"Ow!" I glared at her, but she didn't notice. She was too busy tugging on her rain boots.

"Come on already." She screwed up her face as she tried to squeeze her size-six foot into a size-four pink boot. The boots were cracked around the soles and not a bit waterproof, but they were a Christmas present from two years ago.

She only wore them on whatever she considered a special occasion—anything from Fourth of July fireworks to Mom bringing home a half pint of real imitation maple syrup for weeknight pancakes. I knew something was up if she was willing to suffer pinched toes.

"What do you mean, 'come on'? It's Saturday morning." I struggled to my feet and stood over her with my arms folded, trying to look serious. "I'm hungry. The only place I want to 'come on' to is breakfast."

"We'll eat after." Her foot slipped into the boot with a loud pop.

"I'm hungry now," I said. "Whatever it is, it can wait."

Antonia patted a lumpy towel I'd just noticed was lying next to her. "No, it can't. She can't breathe too good in there."

It wouldn't have taken Sherlock Holmes to figure what was hiding in the towel. I pretended not to care. I'd already decided Antonia had been fooling with me the night before by disguising her voice. Still, the thought of Hush-a-bye being so close made me jittery.

"So what's today?" I asked, staring at the lump under the towel like I was waiting for it to answer.

"You'll see." Antonia giggled. "Big surprise."

I threw on a pair of jeans and a sweatshirt and followed Antonia out of our room. I didn't like it when she played games with secret rules, but I was too tired to argue.

Mom sat hunched on the couch, a steaming mug of instant coffee cradled in both hands. She looked pale and bleary-eyed, like she usually did first thing in the morning. I knew if I spoke fast enough she wouldn't ask too many questions. Antonia had Hush-a-bye towel-wrapped and tucked under one arm.

"Morning, Mom," I said. She nodded weakly. "Antonia found this stale loaf of bread in the road and she brought it in, but I'm going to have her take it outside and break it up and feed the birds and then we'll be right back, okay?"

Mom nodded again. "M'kay, Peppernose," she mumbled.

I don't think she'd heard half of what I'd said. I prodded Antonia in the ribs and mouthed, *Let's go*. She nodded, grinning so hard it made my teeth hurt.

Once outside, Antonia jogged toward the ginkgo tree again. She stopped under it and peered up through the branches.

"Is this all we're out here for?" I was beginning to feel exasperated with Antonia's games. "I told you, it's too early for the leaves to come down."

"Just a second," she said. "I thought I saw one wiggling yesterday." She opened up the towel a little to expose Hush-a-bye's face. "What do think, Hush-a-bye? You think it's time?"

We both glanced at Hush-a-bye like we were expecting her to answer. But her unblinking eyes didn't give any clue what she was thinking about. I shook my head, trying to get rid of the idea that she was thinking anything at all, and craned my neck upward.

The undersides of the ginkgo leaves were pale green against the sky. They didn't look like they were in a hurry to go anywhere any time soon.

"See? Nothing happening today," I said.

"See? Nothing happening today," a high-pitched, mocking voice said.

Icy fingers, cold as February, dug their claws into my sides. I managed to turn my head far enough to see Gus Albero and his friend Zoogie straddling their dirt bikes on my street.

I knew they liked to roam about on their bikes looking for trouble, but I'd never seen them around the trailer park before. I wasn't ready for them. Not here, not now. I wanted to fly down the path behind our trailer, dive right into the water, and dig a tunnel deep under the island.

Zoogie pointed at me with a long, dirty finger. "How about that, Gus?" he said, snickering in his usual weaselly way. "It talks."

The two boys had me trapped. There was nowhere I could disappear to, not with Antonia standing right next to me. My feet felt like they'd been spiked to the ground, and the icy fingers squeezed my brain and made everything look hazy.

"What's that?" Zoogie said, putting a hand to his ear. "Did you say something else?" One thing I knew about Zoogie—if he thought a joke was funny, then repeating it twenty times was hilarious. And me being a silent weirdo was apparently as funny as it got.

"Hi, Gus," Antonia said, oblivious to Zoogie's mocking. She'd hid Hush-a-bye behind her back and rocked on her heels with a big, goofy grin splashed all over her face.

"How about that?" Zoogie said. "The other one talks."

"Of course I can talk," Antonia said. "But I wasn't talking to you."

Gus jerked his head over his shoulder. "Come on, Zoogie. Let's go."

"What are you doing here?" Antonia asked. Gus only gave a microscopic nod in her direction. His eyes quickly darted over to Zoogie to see if even that was noticed.

It suddenly dawned on me that Zoogie was the only one enjoying his jokes. Gus was red-faced and staring at his handlebars. Maybe Gus hadn't realized we lived here, and he didn't want to be stuck in this spot any more than I did.

Antonia had been going on about Gus and the Halloween dance the night before. I'd thought she was making it up in her head. But the way Gus looked like he wanted to stick his head in the ground, it was clear she'd been telling the truth. It was also pretty clear Gus didn't want Zoogie to know anything about it.

Antonia picked up on none of this. She was all misty-eyed and beaming and practically floating two feet off the ground.

"You still going to the Halloween dance?" she asked like someone who thought she already knew the answer.

My brain screamed for Antonia to stop talking, for Gus to grab his stupid friend and ride off on their bikes, or for the river to rise up and crash down on all of us. It screamed and screamed inside my head until I thought my skull was going to split open.

This was going to end badly, I just knew it. But my mouth stayed clamped shut. A six-foot crowbar couldn't pry it open.

Gus just sat like a lump on his bike, squeezing his hand brakes.

"The Halloween dance?" Zoogie asked. His eyes darted from Antonia to Gus with some confusion.

"I said I wasn't talking to you." Antonia gave Zoogie a quick scowl before replacing it with her *for Gus's eyes only* grin. "I'm sure my mom will let me go. It's going to be wicked fun. I hear they're going to decorate the gym with black streamers and real pumpkins and lots of Halloween stuff. Doesn't that sound awesome?"

The light finally blinked on in Zoogie's face. He bounced on his seat and howled with laughter.

Don't, don't, please don't, I begged in my head. It didn't make any difference.

"Gus!" Zoogie squawked. "You didn't tell me you had a girlfriend!"

"Shut up," Gus muttered.

Zoogie kept laughing but in a forced, fake way.

Antonia's grin disappeared. "What's so funny?" she asked.

Gus tried rolling his bike back, but Zoogie grabbed his handlebar and dragged him forward.

"You going to tell me what's so funny, or are you going to keep laughing like a hyena?" Antonia let her arms drop to her sides. One hand still gripped the towel-wrapped head while the other flexed in and out of a fist.

Zoogie snorted. "Maybe I'll keep laughing. What are you holding there?"

Antonia looked down at the bundle in her hand, then quickly pressed it to her chest and folded her arms across it.

"Nothing," she said. "None of your business."

"Maybe I'll make it my business," Zoogie said with a sneer. He started to roll the bike toward us.

Gus shot out an arm and grabbed his wrist. "Knock it off, Zoogie. Let's get out of here."

Zoogie glared at Gus, and then a nasty grin spread across his face. "You protecting your precious girlfriend? That's so sweet."

"Shut up," Gus said.

"Yeah, shut up," Antonia said.

"Aw," Zoogie cooed. "That's too adorable. I bet they crown you king and queen of the dance."

"So what if they do crown us?" Antonia said. "What's it to you?"

Gus's face turned bright red. I could feel what was coming next, how bad it would be. I wanted to step in front of Antonia to protect her, or cinch her to my side and spin the two of us deep underground.

But I didn't. I didn't do anything at all.

Gus slammed his fist against his bike's front reflector, bending it. "Will you stop?" he shouted, his face twisted and ugly. "I'm not taking you to any dance. I never said that. So stop. Just stop."

Antonia stood there with her mouth slightly open, staring ahead like she was trying to find something halfway around the world.

"What?" she said in a thin voice.

"You heard me." Gus straightened his reflector and tried not look at her. Zoogie snickered.

"But—"

"Are you stupid or something?" Zoogie said, slapping his palm against his forehead. "He's not taking you to any dance. What makes you think he'd ask some river rat like you?"

"I'm leaving," Gus said, and turned his bike around.

Zoogie grinned and wiggled his fingers at us. "So long, Queen Ratso," he said, and joined Gus.

I watched Antonia, waiting for her to scream or cry or pick up the largest rock she could find and chuck it at those two idiots. But all she did was bury her face against the towel bundle and pull at her baby-duck barrette. My heart crumbled.

With the boys going, my feet finally unglued from the ground. I shuffled closer to Antonia. Better late than never, I figured, even though I had no idea what to say to her.

As I got nearer, it looked like she was chewing on the towel, which wasn't a good sign. Soon enough she'd start on her nails until they were a ragged mess. She and Mom were both fingernail worriers, and it was a wonder they had any nails left between the two of them. But a closer look showed me she wasn't chewing anything.

She was whispering to Hush-a-bye.

10

I COULDN'T HEAR the words Antonia was saying to Hush-a-bye, but from the way her wet, red-rimmed eyes were glaring, I could guess. And for some reason, it scared me.

"Antonia, don't—"

Before I could get out the words I knew wouldn't do any good, something drew my attention.

Gus and Zoogie were about a hundred feet up the road, facing away from us on their dirt bikes. Their hands gripped their handlebars, and their feet were planted flat on their bike pedals. The strange thing, though, was they weren't moving at all. Their bikes stood upright, perfectly motionless, pinned there like dead bugs on a display board.

The stillness didn't last long. The boys' heads and elbows and shoulders started jerking back and forth. First they jerked just a little, and then their movements grew more frantic.

"My pedals are stuck," Gus said. "Give me a hand, Zoogie."

"I—I can't," Zoogie said. "My hands won't let go."

Gus bounced up and down on his seat like a piston. Zoogie arched his back as if he was trying to lift his whole body in the air. Their hands and feet remained rooted to the bike.

"Somebody put glue on this or something!" Zoogie screamed. He turned his head back as far as he could and bared his teeth at us. "You stupid rat! What did you do?"

Antonia lifted her head from the bundle. "Go ahead and leave." Her voice trembled. "No one's stopping you."

"When I get my hands on—" Zoogie's voice suddenly cut off. The bike wheels had started rolling.

The boys' feet moved with the pedals, but in a strange, uneven way, like some invisible hand was forcing them up and down. The two dirt bikes rolled forward a foot, then circled about slowly, so slowly the bikes should have fallen over. But they didn't.

I stood there shaking. I'd expected the boys to be furious, but their faces were ghost white. Whatever anger they'd stewed in before had been replaced by a feeling that something very bad was about to happen.

"Gus, what's going on?" Zoogie said, all the smirk gone from his voice.

Gus just shook his head back and forth, blinking his eyes rapidly like someone trying to wake from a terrible dream. Their wheels spun a little faster, and the bikes rolled down the road toward Antonia and me. I ran and took hold of her shoulders.

"Let's go," I whispered.

Antonia didn't budge.

"They're going to run us over," I said a little louder, and tried to pull her away.

She shrugged away my grip and planted her feet. "Wait and see."

The bikes were picking up speed. The spokes were spinning so fast they were a blur. The bike wheels smoked, shooting pebbles left and right. They were heading straight in our direction.

Gus bent his head forward and closed his eyes. Zoogie opened his mouth wide. Nothing came out except a strangled whimper.

I wrapped my arms around Antonia as the bikes barreled down on us. I wanted to tell her I was sorry for being such a useless big sister. I wanted to say I should have stood up for her, told those boys to suck eggs or go find the toilet they'd flushed their brains down, told them anything to show them no one could speak to my sister the way they did.

But I didn't say anything. Not one word.

The bikes were so close now I could practically see the little red veins in Zoogie's bulging eyes. I held Antonia tight.

Just as I braced for impact, the two bikes veered off to the side. A rush of air breezed over us as they zoomed past. I felt a thud in my chest when my heart started beating again.

Antonia didn't even flinch.

I twisted around and watched as Gus and Zoogie sped

around our trailer, crashed past the winterberry bushes, and rocketed down the path to the river. Antonia grabbed my hand and yanked me in their direction.

"Come on," she said as I stumbled along behind her like a toddler. "You've got to see this."

An image popped into my head of the two boys speeding straight into the river, flailing and screaming as the water covered their legs, then their shoulders, and finally the tops of their heads. A few bubbles popped along the surface of the water, then stillness.

My stomach lurched.

A howl from behind the tangle of branches and blood-red berries burst the image. We stumbled through and nearly fell out the other side. The howl was joined by a violent whipping sound. It didn't make any sense.

I spotted two pairs of wheel ruts dug deep in the dirt path. They ran parallel for a few feet, then veered left toward a tangle of stinging nettles and pricker bushes.

Several branches were bent and broken. Hanging off one was a thin strip of gray cloth—the same color as Gus's T-shirt.

Antonia, with Hush-a-bye tucked under one arm, clapped her hands and whistled. "Hoo-boy! Hoo-boy!" Now and then she'd sniff and wipe her eyes with the back of her hand.

Careful not to poke ourselves, we pushed aside some pricker branches and peered into the tangle.

Two bikes lay in a heap of weeds. Nearby, the boys thrashed about like rats in a trap.

Thorny vines wrapped around their arms and legs and torsos, and blooms of stinging nettles poked out of holes in their shirts and jeans as if they'd sprouted from the boys' bodies. Their clothes were torn to ribbons, and angry red blotches covered every patch of bare skin.

I couldn't understand how they managed to get themselves wrapped up in the plants so quickly. Then I saw Gus tear off a vine from his leg. As he tossed it far away, another vine snaked along the ground and circled around the same leg. All by itself.

The two boys tore frantically at the nettles and thorns, but something else always reached up and took its place. Like something was trying to keep those boys caught.

"That's impossible," I said.

"Nothing's impossible." Antonia turned to me and smiled. "Not anymore." She bent her head toward the bundled towel and whispered.

All at once, the thrashing stopped.

The branches and vines loosened from the boys' arms and legs and necks and fell away. For a few seconds, they kept grabbing at their limbs like they were still being attacked. But then they stopped and stood staring with pale, blank faces at the piles of broken thorns and smashed nettles.

Antonia pursed her lips and shook her head. "What a mess," she said. "Don't you know not to play in that stuff? I guess you're not so smart yourself, huh?"

Zoogie's face colored a deep red, and his hands balled into tight fists. He started stomping his way toward us. A thorny vine shot out and wrapped itself around his waist. Zoogie was jerked back off his feet. He fell face-first into another bunch of stinging nettles.

"Not smart at all," Antonia said.

Zoogie scrambled to his feet, but before he could try to charge us again, Gus slapped a hand on his chest.

"Get your bike," he said in a low voice. "We're going."

"But—"

"We're going," Gus repeated. There was a definite edge in his words the second time.

Zoogie glared at us, then picked up his bike and pushed it out of the weeds and back up the path. Gus followed. Just before he passed through the winterberry bushes, he glanced back at Antonia with a hangdog look.

Antonia turned her head away. "Go already," she said.

Gus sighed and pushed on through. We could hear the clack of bike pedals and the crunch of tires rolling away. Then nothing.

"Serves them right," Antonia muttered. She unwrapped the doll's head, stroked its curly yellow hair, and kissed its cheek. "Thank you, Hush-a-bye." She kissed it once more and headed down the path toward the river.

I stood there for a long while, looking at the broken plants. Scraps of cloth still clung to thorns here and there,

dotted with tiny specks of blood. The thorny vines and stinging nettles were silent and still. When a gray squirrel suddenly bolted up the side of tree, I waited for something to
reach out and drag it back down. But nothing moved.

Nothing's impossible.

That's what Antonia had said. *Nothing's impossible. Not
anymore.* And I knew it was true.

By the time I reached the riverbank, Antonia was already
sitting there with Hush-a-bye in her lap, the two of them facing the island. Antonia was singing in a quiet, choked voice.

> *Hush-a-bye and good night*
> *Till the bright morning light*
> *Takes the sleep from your eyes*
> *Hush-a-bye, baby bright*

I scrambled down, trying to make as much noise as possible so she'd know I was coming, but she never turned
around.

I sat down next to her, trying to collect all my thoughts
and my breath. Antonia's eyes were still a little red around
the edges, but they were dry. She stroked the doll's hair with
her fingertips. I thought about reaching out to touch her
head, like I wanted to make sure it was real, but a small flutter of fear held me back.

"Did Hush-a-bye do all that up there?" I asked.

Antonia laughed. "She has the best ideas."

"They might have gotten hurt."

Antonia snatched up a handful of pebbles and threw them scattershot into the river. "They got what they deserved." I tried to think of an argument against that, but I couldn't. I had to admit, part of me was glad it happened. At least those boys wouldn't be coming around here again anytime soon.

"And Hush-a-bye got what was coming to her," Antonia continued.

"Huh?"

"I told you. The magic opens up when she can do something to help."

"Right. Like a key," I said, though I really didn't understand. "So what did the key open up for her this time?"

Antonia cocked her head to one side, then held out her arm, extended all her fingers out toward the riverbank, and wiggled them back and forth. "Look," she said.

At first, all I saw was the smooth face of the river, dull and dark under gray clouds that crisscrossed the sky. But then a movement near the grassy edge of the eastern edge of the island caught my eye. Something red with a rounded point was drifting across the water.

At first I thought it might be a big piece of trash someone tossed in the water, like an old tent or a plastic tub. But as it drew closer, I made out the shape of a small rowboat.

It looked empty, as if it hadn't been secured right and had floated away. But something about the way it moved didn't make any sense. The current should have caught that drifting boat and pulled it downstream. Except this boat was headed right for us, slicing through the current like a red-hot knife through a sheet of ice. That was impossible.

Nothing's impossible. Not anymore.

11

THE BOAT GLIDED toward the bank. Antonia waded out to it with Hush-a-bye under one arm and grabbed the prow with her free hand.

"Help me," she said, pulling it closer to the bank. I sloshed into the cold water and took hold of the other side of the boat, and together we pulled it in closer to the riverbank. Two white benches crossed the middle of the boat, and two small white oars lay poking out of the bottom.

"You want to row?" Antonia asked me.

"Row?" I said, blinking. "Row where?"

Antonia rolled her eyes. "To the island. It's waiting for us there."

I don't remember agreeing to anything, yet somehow I found myself sitting in the boat and pulling at the oars, watching as the riverbank drew away. It felt like I was a character in someone else's dream. I wondered if they would ever wake up so all the weirdness would vanish. It was making me a little dizzy.

We reached the big island in the middle of the river and dragged the boat onto the sloped bank. It was thick with yellowing grass, and the pale gray birch trees above it stared down at us silently. Antonia romped up the bank with Hush-a-bye in tow, humming some tuneless song, and quickly disappeared behind the trees. As I watched her, I thought I heard a crowd of voices whispering somewhere deep within the trees. But once I stepped up onto the bank, the voices stopped. I shook my head and followed Antonia.

The ground was covered with dead leaves, ghost-white mushrooms, and small shards of light that somehow managed to get past the thick leaves overhead. Every step I took crackled, but it was the only sound I heard. No birds sang. No flies buzzed. Nothing seemed to live here.

"Come here, Lucy!" Antonia waved to me from behind a stunted tree. Except when I drew closer, I realized it wasn't a dead tree at all. It was a thick, smooth pine post, but darkly discolored like it had been burned. And it wasn't the only one. Several others stuck up from the ground nearby. They were neatly arranged in straight lines, but in various stages of rot and char.

"Someone built a house here?" I said. If they did, it would have been an enormous one, seeing how far along the posts poked up. I spotted a moldy flat pine board lying on the ground between two posts. I could barely make out the letters etched deep into the wood.

LOD

Before I could try to figure out what that could possibly mean, Antonia caught me by the elbow.

"Do you see it?" she squealed, shaking my arm. "Do you?"

I looked at where she was frantically waving her hand. At first, all I saw was a large forked tree. It was long dead, and its branches were curled over like claws. Then I saw what Antonia wanted me to see. She ran to it, and I ran after her.

Propped inside the crook of the tree was a doll-sized yellow dress. It had frills at the shoulders and bottom, and a thin red sash tied around the middle. The style was old-fashioned, like something out of *Anne of Green Gables*, but the dress was spotless and showed no signs of wear.

It also looked weirdly puffed out, like someone had blown it up full of air. Antonia snatched it out of the crook, and I noticed something stuffed inside the dress.

An armless and legless doll's body.

Antonia held it up and gawked at it. "It's beautiful."

She squatted down in the dead leaves and took Hush-a-bye from under her arm. She examined the hole at the bottom of the doll's head and the short knob at the top of the body. She positioned the two together, twisting and turning until there was a sharp snap.

Antonia beamed as she held the limbless doll, stroking

the frills and the sash with her fingertips. She squeezed her tight to her chest and rocked her back and forth.

"Oh, Hush-a-bye, Hush-a-bye," she said, kissing her on the nose. "You found your body. I'm so happy for you." And then she turned away from me and headed back to the island slope without another word.

I shut my eyes and played back the scenes in my brain— the way the two boys were attacked by the stinging nettles and thorny vines, and how the strange little rowboat brought us to the island to find Hush-a-bye's body. I also thought about the exploding milk in the school cafeteria and the bright green eye that somehow found its way to the ginkgo tree.

Nothing's impossible. Not anymore. The words came back to me once again. Except now I really believed them. Like Dorothy in Oz, I sure couldn't pretend we were still in Kansas.

Once we returned to our side of the river, I hid the rowboat in some thick undergrowth and covered it with branches. It seemed wrong to leave it there, like it was evidence of . . . I don't what. Then I ran after Antonia.

When I finally caught up with her at the winterberry bushes, my chest burned like I'd swallowed a jar of pickled jalapeños. "Hold up for a second and let me catch my breath," I said.

Antonia had plucked off a handful of the red berries. She rolled them around her palm, then picked them up one at a time and squished them between her fingers.

"I wasn't making it up when I said Gus asked me if I was going to the dance," she said as she pinched a particularly fat berry. "I remember what he said. I'm not stupid."

I shuffled my feet. Something about the tone of her voice prickled my skin. "I believe you, Antonia."

Antonia dropped the rest of the berries on the ground. "He lied to me." She scowled at the berries scattered on the dirt path. "I hate it when people lie to me. So does Hush-a-bye. She says two-faced deceivers—that's what she calls liars—she says those kind of people deserve everything bad that comes to them." She lifted her boot and stomped the berries into a messy red pulp. She looked straight at me, and I felt my throat tighten. "You'd never lie to me, Lucy. Would you?" she asked.

I tried to smile. "Of course not," I lied.

12

THE NEXT TIME we saw Gus and Zoogie, they were shuffling down the aisle of the school bus. They kept their eyes fixed on the back seats and never said a word to us.

As they passed by, Antonia pretended to suddenly find her fingernails extremely fascinating. But as Gus slumped his way past, I caught Antonia giving him a quick, sidelong glance.

The rest of the week drifted by like any other school week, no better or worse, although Mr. Capp did make an announcement during Wednesday's class about an after-school art club.

"It'll give a chance for those of you who want to flex their creative muscles"—he pumped his arms up like a bodybuilder while the class giggled—"to do stuff we don't have time for in regular class. The first meeting will be in a few weeks. If you're interested, you can let me know ahead of time. Or just show up. Everybody's welcome."

May turned to me, grinning so hard I thought she might break a few teeth. "I'm definitely going. How about you? It'll be a lot of fun."

All I offered back was a noncommittal shrug and a quiet "I'll think about it." But I'd already made up my mind. The idea of spending more time at school and taking an unfamiliar late bus home with God-knows-who was more than I could handle.

Antonia still had her nightly talks with Hush-a-bye. What they talked about, she never said. Then again, she wasn't saying much to me at all anymore.

It wasn't like she was rude or angry or giving me dirty looks. But it felt like the bond that held us together was stretching thinner and thinner every day. I was starting to worry one day it might snap and leave me alone on one side and her and Hush-a-bye on the other. When I thought back on all those wishes I'd made over the years to be an only child, and how those wishes were mocking me now—it scared me.

At our usual Friday-night family dinner, Mom announced that for the first time in ages, she had the weekend off. She explained the restaurant she worked at was going to be closed for fumigation. When Antonia asked what "fumigation" meant, Mom just shuddered and changed the subject, suggesting we talk about what we could do with the extra time. But before either me or Antonia could rattle off the hundred ideas that popped into both our heads, Mom declared we'd use the time to clean up the trailer, starting with what she referred to as the sorry state of our room.

Her biggest concern was the underside of Antonia's bed, which Mom insisted would require a pickax and a couple of sticks of dynamite to clear out. Antonia protested and grumbled for a few minutes like she always did when the subject of any kind of cleaning came up, but like always, she knuckled under Mom's unblinking glare.

By the time we were done cleaning, our bedroom looked like—well, it still looked like a dumpy little bedroom in a ratty old trailer, but at least it was cleaner. As a reward, Mom brought out a whole lemon meringue pie she'd gotten from work earlier in the week and hidden behind a head of lettuce. It was a little stale, but we ate the whole thing up, crumbs and all, and we went to bed with full, happy bellies.

That night, I wondered if I was worrying too much for my own good. Nothing weird had happened since the whole mess with Gus and Zoogie. Maybe that was the end of that, I told myself. Hush-a-bye had gotten her body and her dress back after all. Sure, she didn't have arms or legs, but what did a doll really need them for anyway? And even though her best friend was a doll she talked to in the closet, Antonia seemed to be adjusting to regular school better than expected. Certainly better than I ever did.

Now I felt silly for worrying about her drifting away. So what if Antonia talked more to Hush-a-bye than me lately? It didn't mean it would always be like that. She'd come around eventually and want to talk to someone who actually talks back, and everything would fall back into place. My life wouldn't be better, but it wouldn't be any worse. I could live with that.

But then Monday morning came, and the bottom fell out of everything.

It happened in social studies, in the last twenty minutes of class. Our teacher, Ms. Crozzetti, stood in front of us and removed her glasses. That got everyone's attention. Usually, when those glasses came off, a stern lecture was sure to follow.

It wasn't clear what the lecture would be about. The class had been pretty low-key for the most part—no one sneaking out cell phones, no boys making fart noises with their hands, no stupid time-wasting questions. Also, Ms. Crozzetti was actually smiling, a thing so rare there were rumors she wasn't able to due to a freak accident during a triple root canal.

"I've got a surprise for you today," Ms. Crozzetti said. "Actually, the surprise is one week from tomorrow, but I'm going to tell you about it today. It's about a special field trip. How many of you have been to Old Hops Village?"

She stood there beaming at us for a few seconds. The wall of silence she ran into forced her glasses back on her face.

"For those of you who don't know," she said in a disgusted tone, as if not knowing was only slightly better than being a nose picker, "Old Hops Village is an authentic historical re-creation of a nineteenth-century village about thirty miles north of us. It also happens to align perfectly with our upcoming unit on postcolonial life in New York State."

"So it isn't a fun trip?" someone said from the back of the room.

The glasses came off again, but this time Ms. Crozzetti had her lecture face on. "I'll have you know I've spent the past two months writing up a grant to pay for this field trip, which *I thought* would be a nice change of pace from reading the textbook. But if you'd rather stay put and do that . . ." She waited for a response, knowing full well no one wanted that option, then re-glassed herself and opened her plan book.

"Now, while this is a field trip, it is also an educational trip, which means you will have an assignment to do while you're there." She ignored the groans piling up around the room and pulled out a thick packet.

"You will be working with a partner *that I will choose*"—more groans—"to complete this packet as you visit the differ-ent sites around the museum. And just so there's no wonder-ing and fussing about who's going to be with whom, I'll tell you who your partner's going to be right now."

Icy fingers crawled up my spine as Ms. Crozzetti con-sulted her plan book. A partner? Who I'd have to work with? Why didn't she just borrow a hammer from the custodian and split my head open? It would have been a lot less painful.

As she read the paired names, I tried to imagine who'd

be the least awful partner. Ellie Vance was almost as quiet as I was. And Priya Kaur seemed friendly enough, even if she'd never said anything to me.

Not that my opinion mattered. The names had already been written out, and Ms. Crozzetti was the kind of teacher who wouldn't change a list unless someone dropped dead, and even then she'd be seriously annoyed about the inconvenience. The only thing I could hope for was she wouldn't make the torture worse by partnering me with the one person I dreaded more than a long and violently painful death.

And the moment I thought it, I knew it was going to happen.

"Lucy Bloom," Ms. Crozzetti said as the icy fingers squeezed themselves around my throat, "you'll be partners with Maddie Underwood."

Maddie Underwood. *Madison.*

It was all I could do to keep from falling out of my chair and collapsing in a quivering heap. This was bad— end-of-the-world zombie apocalypse kind of bad. Well, maybe not *that* bad, but it was a pretty close second.

I managed to steal a glance toward the front of the class, where Madison sat. She never turned to look back at me, didn't moan and carry on, didn't even turn to one of the Oslo twins to roll her eyes. But she'd never do that in front of the teacher. She'd never let any adult see behind her perfect mask.

Ms. Crozzetti finished her list and asked if there were any questions. A smirking boy raised his hand.

"Yes, Marty?" Ms. Crozzetti said, pinching the top of her nose and closing her eyes.

"Can we stop for ice cream on the way back? That would be awesome."

Ms. Crozzetti sighed. "Any *useful* questions?"

Madison raised her hand. I stiffened. Was she going to ask for a new partner? The thought of it gave me a little thrill of hope, even as I braced for the humiliation.

"Ms. Crozzetti," Madison said in her sweetest classroom voice, "will there be any extra credit?"

13

I WAITED FOR the hammer to drop. The hammer, of course, was Madison, who I was sure couldn't wait to let Ashley and Gretta Oslo know how disgusted she was having me as a partner.

With my head bent low, and the icy fingers twisting my stomach in knots, I slunk out of social studies and waited for poison to rain down on me.

"Can you believe you got Trash Licker of all people?" started Gretta, not wasting a moment.

Here we go, I thought. *Just get it over with.*

Madison didn't respond right away. I figured she was thinking of something especially nasty, something that would outnasty all the other horrible things she'd ever said to me.

"Gretta," she said finally, and I braced myself. "Where did you get your nails done? They look so awesome."

I almost stopped in the middle of the hallway. *Nails?* Must have been a fake-out. She'd drop the bomb on me soon enough.

Even Gretta was thrown off balance. "My . . . my nails? What, these? Do you think so?"

"Oh yeah," Madison said. "I can't stand this glossy neon stuff I've been wearing. I mean, look at it. Yuck."

And all the way to science, Madison and Ashley and Gretta talked nails. Nothing but nails.

It wasn't a one-day fluke either. The insult shutout continued for the rest of the week. On the endless three-minute trudge from social studies to science, the three of them talked about how Mrs. Burns, the PE teacher, had the nerve to lecture the girls about proper dental care, considering her own crooked, mossy teeth; if it were true eating Pop Rocks and drinking Coke at the same time would make your stomach explode; why seventh-grade boys acted like such cheeseheads whenever three or more of them got together; and so on and so on.

You'd have thought I'd be relieved not to be her daily punching bag. But I wasn't. My nerves were stretched out like thin wires of brittle glass.

The hammer might have looked like it was gone, but I knew it was only in hiding, waiting for just to right moment to strike. And when Madison finally brought it back out and walloped me, it would break me in pieces so small I'd never be put back together.

On Thursday, our social studies class met in the library to research postcolonial life in New York for the field trip the following week.

Ms. Crozzetti piled a stack of books on one of the library floor shelves. She instructed us to pick one book, check it out at the library desk, read it (she repeated this part three times), and write a short paragraph highlighting a detail about daily life.

I darted ahead of the crowd, snatched the nearest book, and was the first one in line at the library desk. Once I checked it out, I made my way to a library table separated from all the others. Just like the cafeteria, I knew the best places in every part of the school to keep out of sight.

After kids stopped scrambling for books and friends to sit with, the librarian quit shushing, and Ms. Crozzetti barked out her final-warning detention threats, the library quieted down to the low buzz of the fluorescent lights. I let out a breath and took my first look at the book I'd taken.

Hunter's Moon Island: A History.

I stifled a yawn. Not exactly a thrill ride of a book. It even smelled old and musty. On the other hand, boredom was better than fretting about Madison and her secret evil plans for me, so I set my chin on my hand and got ready to flip open the cover. But a voice stopped my hand.

"Hey, Lucy."

My heart squeezed up tight like it usually did when anyone talked to me. Then I looked up and saw May Darasavath standing there with an armful of books. Immediately I relaxed.

"Hi," I said.

"Look at all the new Demon Donnie books that came in!" She grinned and displayed her book treasure. "They're mostly about what happens between episodes or in alternate universes, so they're not really canon, but they're still pretty awesome. You here with Ms. Crozzetti's class?" I nodded, and May nodded with me. "My friend Richie, who knows everything about everything, says she's doing a field trip. That sounds so cool! I wish I was going." She let out a dramatic sigh. "But I got Mr. Bradley for social studies. He's so boring."

A loud "Shh!" came from behind one of the bookshelves. May rolled her eyes and bent in closer to speak to me. "I bet you have partners. Richie says Ms. Crozzetti loves doing partners. Who's yours?"

"Madison . . . Maddie Underwood," I said, trying to sound like I didn't care.

May frowned. "That's too bad."

"Too bad?"

"Yeah. I know her. She's in my math class. I guess she's supposed to be smart, but she's got a mean streak she doesn't let the teachers see. I wouldn't want her as a partner. Yuck. Still, I kind of feel a little sorry for her."

I stared at May. Sorry for her? For Madison? Perfect, poisonous Madison? How was that possible? I had to ask.

"Why are you sorry for her?"

May's face turned serious, which wasn't something I'd seen from her. "She tries so hard to be popular. It must be exhausting."

I kept staring at May. I'd always thought of Madison as a girl who skated through life without a care, shoving away all obstacles—such as me—without missing a beat. It never occurred to me she might be skating on thin ice, terrified of the frigid water below her feet.

But before I could say anything about that (which wasn't too likely), May grinned and said, "Anyway, it's just one day, so I wouldn't worry about it. I better let you get back to work before I get you in trouble. Keep thinking about Art Club. Bye!" She wiggled her fingers at the top of her book stack and left.

If my brain wasn't in a muddle before, now it was a thick pea soup of confusion. May saw the nastiness hiding under Madison's perfect smile, but she still felt sorry for her. And that made me wonder if maybe Madison really was exhausted from playing all her petty little games to show how much better she was than a little nothing like me. Maybe she was bored of the whole Trash Licker thing and had moved on from harassing me to just pretending I didn't exist. I could live with that.

Then again, could I really afford to let my guard down?

I closed my eyes and shook my head. It was too, too much to take in, and I didn't really want to take a deep dive into my thoughts about Maddie right then. So I planted my chin in my hands once more and opened the Hunter's Moon Island book. And when I saw the photograph of the island printed on the first page, I sat up.

"That's our island," I whispered under my breath.

It was unmistakable. I'd looked at it practically every day over summer vacation. The same birch trees and the same puzzle-piece curve of the shore.

Who knew it had a name? Who knew it had a history?

I flipped through the pages looking for more pictures of the island, skimming through the sections on early Oneida settlements and European explorers of the Susquehanna, until I stopped at a photograph under a chapter titled "Hunter's Moon Lodge: A Hotel Island Dream." Faded and scratched, the photo showed a long white two-story building with rows of windows and columns dotted along both floors and a large sign on top reading HUNTER'S MOON LODGE.

I thought back to the day last week that Antonia and I had found Hush-a-bye's body on the island. I remembered the charred pine columns set in a row and the pine board with the letters *LOD* I'd discovered in the dead leaves. I shivered, but I kept reading.

I read that fifteen years after the end of the Civil War, a steamboat company ran river tours up and down the Susquehanna River with a stop at Hunter's Moon Island, a perfect spot to let the tourists out to stretch their legs and have a picnic. It became such a popular destination, some-one decided to build a hotel there.

"Of all things," I muttered. "A hotel on a river island."

I turned the page to read more about the hotel, and I saw another photograph with the caption *Hunter's Moon Lodge, Summer 1881*. I stared at the picture taken almost a hundred and forty years ago, and icy fingers dragged slowly down my spine.

It was an old-fashioned black-and-white photo, the kind where the black is washed out and almost looks brown. In it, a girl my age stood stiffly in front of a forked tree. She wore what seemed to be a gingham dress, and her face was expres-sionless, like a mask.

But it wasn't her name or her lack of expression or the familiar forked tree that made me feel like all the air had been sucked out of the room. It was the doll she cradled in her arms. The curly, light-colored hair, the dress with frills at the end of the sleeves and along the bottom, and the thin dark sash tied above her waist—I'd seen it all before.

Hush-a-bye.

But it wasn't possible. It didn't make any sense.

Nothing's impossible. Not anymore.

Above the photograph was a title: *A Hunter's Moon Lodge Mystery.* I chewed the end of my pencil in my mouth furi-ously, my fingers tracing the last word. I was so caught up in what the mystery might be, I never heard her approach.

"Hey, Lucy."

I thought at first May had come back to gab a little more, which was okay by me. But it sure didn't sound like May's voice. I glanced up.

It wasn't May standing there.

It was Madison.

I snapped the book shut. Madison stood by the library table with a smile on her face. My mind raced. *What is she doing? Why did she call me Lucy?* I didn't even think she knew my real name.

She pulled back a chair and sat down next to me. The pencil still dangled from my mouth.

Madison opened up a bright yellow binder and took out a neon yellow sheet of paper. She smoothed it on the table with her nicely manicured fingers and pushed it over to me.

Extra Credit Project (+10 points): Madison Underwood and Lucy Bloom was typed in bold face across the top.

"I've been thinking about the extra credit we could do at Old Hops Village," she said breezily, as if this conversation was something we did every day. "I went online and looked at the different exhibits they have there, and I thought it would be cool to do one on the Gypsum Man. Have you heard of that?"

My pencil decided right then to fall onto the table with a loud clatter. Madison glanced down at it briefly, and a flicker of annoyance crossed her face. Then she twisted her smile back on and continued.

"So the Gypsum Man was this big hoax, like, about a hundred years ago. There was this guy who made this big stone man and buried it and convinced a whole bunch of people for a while that the Gypsum Man was this for-real ancient giant. They have a special exhibit at the Village about the Gypsum Man, so I thought it would make a good extra credit project, don't you think?"

"Uh, sure," I mumbled.

Madison, looking very pleased, stuck the paper back in her binder. "Don't worry about doing anything now," she said as she pushed back her chair and stood. "We'll take notes when we're there, and then afterward we'll figure out what to do with them. Okay, see you later."

And just like that, she was gone.

14

AFTER MADISON LEFT, I just sat there, staring into the air, thinking about the one-sided conversation I'd had with her.

She'd called me Lucy. Not Trash Licker. Lucy. And she asked for my help with a project. Had she changed? Or was she setting me up? Or maybe she was being nice because of the project, schoolwork being the one thing she was dead serious about. Maybe once it was all over I'd go back to being Trash Licker again.

Maybe. Maybe not. I didn't have a clue.

When the period bell rang, I absentmindedly stuffed *Hunter's Moon Island* in my bag and slunk off to the next class.

For the rest of the day I wandered through a thick fog. I didn't hear a word any of my teachers spoke. Somehow, I managed to get on the right bus and find my way home. Antonia had to stay after school for some extra tutoring in reading, so I rode alone. It wouldn't have mattered if she was there. She could have straddled my shoulders and bopped me on the head with a sock full of cat litter and I wouldn't have noticed.

Mom's car wasn't parked by the trailer, so I was on my own. I drank a glass of water and ate a sleeve of stale crackers Mom brought home from Theodora's diner sometime last week. I turned on the TV but got nothing but fuzz, so I turned it off and went to my room.

I tossed my bag down and sat on the edge of my bed. The closet door was wide open. I could see the little wooden chair Antonia sat on each night. At the edge of the doorway, the frilly lace of a small yellow dress peeked out. My fingers dug deep into my blanket. I sat there for the longest time, chewing on an idea that was either amazingly brilliant or completely insane.

"Why not?" I finally said, and I got off the bed.

I clicked on the single bulb in the closet and eased myself carefully on the chair, not sure if it would hold me as well as Antonia. It creaked a little, but otherwise seemed pretty solid.

Hush-a-bye's green eyes gleamed in the dull yellow light of the closet, like they had their own flame buried somewhere deep inside. I cleared my throat.

"So," I started, "I think you know I'm Antonia's sister, Lucy. I'm sure you've seen me around."

I waited a moment. The doll said nothing. That was

probably for the best, because if she started talking back, I would have screamed for sure.

"Anyway, all those things you did for Antonia—I really don't know how you did them—they were pretty awesome. The thing is, I was wondering if this was an exclusive thing between you and Antonia, or if you could help someone else out, maybe?"

I ran my fingers through my hair and bit my bottom lip.

"Okay, so there's this girl at my school—her name is Madison—and she's real pretty but she's not always so pretty inside. Not to me, anyway. Lately she's been nicer to me, but I wonder if she's just pretending. Whatever it is, I'm worried about this field trip coming up on Tuesday, where I'm her partner. I'm scared she's going to try and do something mean to me."

Just talking about it made my chest tighten. I breathed slowly in through my nose and out through my mouth, which I'd read somewhere was a good way to calm yourself down.

"So I guess what I'm asking is . . . is . . . I don't know what I'm asking. I mean, I can't tell anyone else about it. Well, I could, but I can't, if you know what I mean."

I reached out and touched Hush-a-bye's blond curls. They were so soft and silky, and I stroked them with the back of my hand.

"Can you help me?" I said.

I don't know how long I sat there, staring into her green eyes, waiting for an answer. Eventually, I heard the front door of the trailer open, so I stood and turned off the light, and I quietly closed the closet door behind me.

Before I left the room, I pressed my ear against the door and closed my eyes. But inside the closet, it was still and silent.

When the morning of the field trip finally came, I went through the motions of getting ready. My head was lost in a bubbling stew of fear and confusion. Somehow I managed to dress myself for school and get out the door, though I didn't remember doing any of it.

The sky was thick with dark, brooding clouds. A slight breeze shivered the leaves of the ginkgo. They were yellowing now, but the ground at its trunk was still untouched by fallen leaves.

"Hurry up!" Antonia yelled. She was already waiting at the bus stop.

"Wait! I forgot something," I yelled back, and before Antonia could complain, I ran back into the trailer. I dashed into our room, unzipping my bag along the way, and threw open the closet door.

Before I could change my mind, I pulled Hush-a-bye off the cardboard box. I laid her in the bottom of my bag and covered her up with a couple of notebooks and the bag lunch Mom packed for the field trip. Then I slammed the door shut and raced back as quickly as I could, my heart beating so hard I thought the whole world could hear it.

15

"LISTEN UP! LISTEN up!" Ms. Crozzetti banged her clipboard and stomped her feet on the bus aisle floor until the last bit of conversation was crushed under her stony glare.

"You all should have your packets and your maps of the village. From ten thirty to noon, you need to make sure you visit at least three buildings and write down three specific facts you learned from each one. At noon, we will meet at the village green for lunch. *Do not be late.* After that, you'll have forty-five minutes to explore on your own and then at one thirty—*exactly one thirty*—the bus is leaving. With or without you. *Capisce?*"

"Ca-what?"

"Do you understand?"

No one admitted to not understanding, so we were let off the bus. It was a relief to finally stretch my legs. I'd been sitting like a block of ice for an hour, pretending to look at whatever was passing outside the bus window.

The sky was slate-colored, and the air felt damp, but the rain had held off. Good thing too. I'd only packed a cheap plastic poncho Mom got from the dollar store. With any luck I wouldn't have to pull it out. I'd have to be careful getting anything out of my bag so no one would see Hush-a-bye.

I'd regretted bringing her the moment I stepped on the bus. What was I thinking? What made me think she'd help me at all? And what kind of help was I looking for anyway? Worst of all, if anyone found out I was carrying a legless, armless doll around, I'd be marked the rest of my life as something worse than Trash Licker. Especially if Madison found out.

"Come on, Lucy," Madison said once we piled off the bus and Ms. Crozzetti threatened us one more time. "We're going to visit the blacksmith first."

Madison smiled at me with brilliant white teeth. Even in the middle of this dull gray day, she shone like a new penny. I couldn't find a hint of poison in her copper-brown eyes.

Could I be wrong about her? I wondered. *I mean, after I threw up on her desk, did I ever say I was sorry? Maybe she thought I hated her. And now she's giving me a second chance. People do change. Occasionally.* Warily, I let the icy fingers clutching my spine melt a little. *Very* little, since Ashley and Gretta were joining us, and I still didn't exactly trust Madison.

At the blacksmith shop, a sweaty man in a thick apron heaved a bellows until the iron bar he held turned a fiery, angry red. He banged and twisted and hammered the end of the bar until it became a sharp black nail. Then he snapped it off with a quick motion. After dousing it in a bucket of water to cool off, he offered it to Gretta. She giggled and accepted it.

"What am I supposed to do with one nail?" asked Gretta with a pout as we walked out of the shop. She looked over her shoulder quickly, then dropped it to the ground.

I thought about scooping it up and taking it home for Antonia, but there were too many kids around. I didn't want to become the girl who picked up trash and put it in her pocket. It would be just the kind of thing Madison would say I'd do. Or she used to, anyway.

From there we visited a one-room schoolhouse with a potbellied wood stove and tiny, cramped desks that made my butt sore just looking at them.

"This is the whole school?" Ashley asked, sniffing at a row of old books. "That's so weird."

"Totally weird," Gretta agreed.

"I don't know," Madison said. She looked dreamily at one of the desks and trailed her manicured nail against it. "My father told me he used to go to a one-room schoolhouse back in South Dakota when he was a kid. He liked it."

"No way!" Ashley said. "Did he really? That is so bizarro! Why did he do a thing like that?"

A flash of anger brightened Madison's eyes for a brief moment, and then she smiled as she set her hand on the potbellied wood stove in the center of the classroom.

"I'd hate to be the one who had to sit next to this," she

said, ignoring Ashley's question. "All that heat would murder my hair."

"Do you think?" Ashley asked, twirling a strand of her own hair. I couldn't tell if she'd already forgotten her other question, or if she'd seen the look in Madison's eye and decided to let it drop.

We moved on to the general store. A sweet, spicy smell of ginger and lemon drops filled the room. It was stocked with candies, lumps of soap, marbles, and Jacob's ladders. Madison bought a bottle of eucalyptus oil. The twins split a bag of licorice. I didn't have any money, but I pretended to browse until the girls were done making their purchases.

We ended up on the green lawn in front of an old-time tavern. Most of the class was already parked in small groups along the grass. They rustled paper lunch bags and jabbered like mice.

Madison and the Oslo twins sat in a tight circle, talking more than eating, but at least not about me. Not about anything, really. I sat next to them, like the tail on a Q, and listened.

I was in the middle of chewing a big bite of meat-loaf sandwich Mom had brought me from the diner when I realized a strange thing. It had snuck up on me bit by bit. But once I recognized it, I stopped chewing. Was it really possible?

The icy fingers had slipped away. More than that, I suspected there was a small chance I was enjoying myself. Sort of.

Now, Madison and Ashley and Gretta and me hadn't

exactly been all buddy-buddy. I hadn't magically broken free of my shell either. I hadn't said a word to any of them, and they hadn't tried to speak to me all that much. But we walked together and filled out our packet questions together and gawked at the displays together and ate our lunches together. And through it all, not one unpleasant word about me wormed its way out of any of their mouths.

It wasn't exactly friendship, but it was as close as I'd been to it so far at this school, except for May. I swallowed my sandwich and watched the three girls move effortlessly in and out of each other's conversations. It was so easy for them, and it dawned on me how much I'd been missing.

I wanted to be that way—one of them. I wanted to laugh and talk about silly, pointless things. I wanted it more than anything.

I looked over to them with a little bit of hope warming me. Their heads were clustered together tightly, and I could not hear what they were saying, though I could hear Ashley giggling about something. I leaned in slightly to see if I could catch their conversation. But before I could, they broke apart and Madison turned around. She gave a start, like she wasn't expecting I'd be looking right at her, then eased into a smile.

"Are you ready, Lucy?" Madison said. I blinked and stared stupidly at her. "Remember? The extra credit project about the Gypsum Man. It's not too far from here."

"Uh, yeah," I managed to mumble, and tucked my half-eaten lunch into my bag, careful not to reveal Hush-a-bye.

Why did I bring her here? I thought to myself. *Grow up already.*

The Gypsum Man display was in a large, candy-striped shack. It was set back from the village at the foot of a low hill dotted with spiny shrubs. Next to the door was a large white sign.

THE GYPSUM MAN

TWELVE FEET, NINE AND ONE-HALF INCHES TALL

THREE THOUSAND AND FIVE HUNDRED POUNDS

TALLER THAN GOLIATH, WHOM DAVID CONQUERED WITH A SINGLE STONE

"So . . . is this a real giant?" Gretta asked, wrinkling her nose. "I bet it's not."

"Twelve feet's kind of short for a giant," Ashley said, and snorted. "I thought he was going to be like a hundred feet or something. He's puny."

"I already explained this," Madison said with a sigh. She pulled out a folded sheet of green paper. "What I found out is that about a hundred years ago there was a guy who came up with the idea of carving a big piece of gypsum stone to make this giant, and then he buried it in a place where he knew someone would dig it up and find it."

"That's stupid," Gretta said. "What did he do that for?"

"Because whoever dug it up would think they'd discovered the body of some lost race of giant people, and this guy who'd had it buried in the first place would make a fortune charging people to look at it. People love looking at weird stuff."

"I bet he made a lot of money," Ashley said. "My cousin Rachel once got two hundred dollars online for a baby-Jesus chimichanga."

"Did not," Gretta said, wagging her finger. "It was a burrito. A *frozen* burrito."

"Whatever."

Madison cleared her throat loudly. "So *anyway*, they figured out pretty quickly it was a fake. But he did end up selling it for a few thousand dollars. Let's go look." Madison turned to me and smiled. "Come on, Lucy. He won't bite."

"I . . . I sure hope not," I said, and offered up a thin smile. I cringed a little at my lame attempt at a joke, but Madison didn't roll her eyes at me or make a face, so it almost felt like we'd made a tiny connection. It was a start, anyway.

Inside was a single, brightly lit room. The walls were covered with large black-and-white photographs from a long time ago. A few small round tables were scattered about the room with uncomfortable-looking metal chairs pushed under them.

In the center of the room was an enormous box resting on a black marble pedestal. White-painted wooden steps surrounded three sides of the box.

"Creepy," Ashley said.

I had to agree. We all stood there scuffing our sneakers on the floor. Then Madison groaned.

"It's only a big dude-shaped rock," she said. "Let's go already."

Madison strode up the long middle steps. Ashley and Gretta followed sheepishly behind her. I shuffled toward the far end of the box and crept one step at a time. We all reached the top step together and looked inside. Gretta shrieked and covered her mouth.

"No . . . way," Ashley said. She drew the words out in a long, breathy rasp, rapping her palm against her chest after each one. "He's naked!"

The Gypsum Man was laid out in what looked like an open cement coffin. He looked like a big dude-shaped rock, just like Madison said. He was also very, very naked.

My face grew hot, and I tried to look up at the hanging lights. I didn't dare move away while the girls were still there. I didn't want to look ridiculous.

"Now look what you've done, Ashley," Madison said. "You've embarrassed Lucy."

And there it was.

The familiar mocking tone, the one Madison usually used to trash-talk me in the hallway. It had found its way back into her voice.

My hands gripped the edge of the box. I should have known it was too good to be true. I'd let my guard down. And now I was all alone with the three of them. *Idiot!*

I braved a look at the girls. They were huddled together, whispering with their hands over their mouths, glancing at me now and then. The friendly masks they'd been wearing were gone, and their glances were full of bad intentions.

Especially Madison's. I knew those eyes well. I could practically smell the poison in them.

The icy fingers returned with a vengeance. They squeezed themselves tight around my throat.

Madison strolled over to me. Ashley and Gretta followed close behind, giggling. I tried to move down the steps, but Madison hopped over quickly and placed her hand on the small of my back.

"Not so fast." She shoved me to the top of the stairs.

I didn't try to resist, even though my legs felt like rubber. I grabbed the railing again.

Madison laid a cold hand over mine. I couldn't stop trembling.

"You like him, don't you?" Madison whispered. She pulled at my fingers and peeled them away from the railing.

"I bet she wants to kiss him," Gretta said. She stood at my left side and pried my other hand away. Ashley giggled from behind.

"See her shaking? She can't wait," Madison said. I could feel her hot breath in my ear. "You two were made for each other. He's an ugly Trash Licker—just like you."

Madison yanked my hand and grabbed hold of my arm. Gretta wrenched the bag off my back and tossed it across the floor. Then she lunged for my legs while Ashley grabbed my other arm.

I squirmed and twisted as they lifted me off the steps, but I couldn't loosen their grip.

I wanted to scream. I wanted to howl at the top of my lungs and spit in their faces and batter them with every curse word I'd ever heard.

I wanted to—but I didn't.

They carried me, silently thrashing, to the front of the box. They propped me on the edge of it, and then they shoved me over the side.

My hands flailed wildly as I fell. The air was sucked out of my lungs. I scraped my palms and knees against the rough surface of the Gypsum Man's torso. Sharp pains shot through them, and I cried out.

"How about that?" Madison said. "Trash Licker finally said something."

"She must be hot for her new boyfriend," Ashley said, and they all laughed.

For the longest time, I stayed there on my hands and knees, staring into the blank face of the stone man. My whole body shook like there was an earthquake right below me. My stomach lurched. I thought I was going to puke. I closed my eyes and bit the inside of my cheek until the feeling passed.

I slowly turned one hand up. It was covered in dust and blood. I lifted my knees, ignoring the stabbing pains inside them, and tucked my feet underneath. My hair had fallen in front of my face, drenched with sweat. I pulled my wet bangs aside.

Madison stood there with her phone. A light flashed, and she showed the pic she'd taken to Ashely and Gretta. I half wondered if their high-pitched laughter would shatter the windows. I wished it would. I wished it bring the walls and whole ceiling down and crush us all.

"Can you send me that pic?" Gretta asked as I slid off the giant and hobbled to the far side of the box.

"Oh, I'm going to send them to *everyone*," Madison said, "but first I'm—"

"No way!" Ashley shrieked.

I'd managed to climb over the side of the box and was slowly making my way down the steps when I saw what Ashley was hollering about. Before I saw it, I'd felt like a lamb after being attacked by a pack of wild dogs. I may have been bloodied and mangled, but the dogs already had their fill of me, so at least the worst of it was over.

Once again, I was wrong.

There was always something worse. Always.

And there it was in front of me.

The three girls stood openmouthed in a half circle around my open bag. And dangling from Ashley's hand was the limbless body of Hush-a-bye.

16

A COUPLE OF years ago, Mom took Antonia and me to a prehistoric exhibit at a science museum. Along with the trilobite fossils and the plaster T. rex jaw, there was a display of tiny insects that had been trapped in amber millions of years ago. They didn't look dead suspended in that smooth brown glassiness. Just stuck in a single moment forever.

I knew how they felt now, because I was rooted to the spot near the Gypsum Man exhibit like a bug in amber. If a wrecking ball had come crashing through the wall and headed straight at me, I couldn't have budged an inch.

Ashley's painted fingers were twisted through Hush-a-bye's long blond curls. The doll's body swayed gently back and forth. Her green eyes, even from across the room, shone bright. I watched them staring back at me like we were the only ones in the room.

But the spell between us didn't last. Once Madison spoke, everything came back into focus.

"I thought Trash Licker was just a name everyone called you," Madison said, her lips curling in a sneer. "Turns out it you really are a Trash Licker."

"Ew! Ew!" Ashley shrieked. "Take it, Gretta. I don't want to hold it."

Gretta backed away and waved her hands. "No way! That thing is probably full of lice."

Ashley screamed and shook her fingers until Hush-a-bye came loose. The doll crashed to the floor.

"Ew! Gross!" Ashley made a big show of shivering from head to toe. "Now I have to go wash my hands. Gretta, come with me. Please!"

Gretta rolled her eyes. "Fine. You coming, Maddie?"

Madison shook her head and smiled. "Think I'll get a few pics of Trash Licker's nightmare doll and send them out with the other ones. Meet you back at the green."

"Okay. Bye-bye, Trash Licker!"

"Yeah, so long, weirdo."

The twins ran out, squealing and giggling, leaving the door halfway open. Madison picked up the doll by its neck. She pinched the frills and poked at the eyes. Then she turned Hush-a-bye around, and her eyes widened.

"Pretty," she said as she undid the red sash around the dress. She gave me a glance, smirked, and stuffed the sash in her pants pocket. Then she placed the doll on the steps leading up to the Gypsum Man's box and clicked away with her phone.

I stood there and let her do it. Like I always did. Except this time she'd found a way to grind me under her heel in front of the whole school.

I could hear them already, pointing at me and laughing until their faces turned red. The Trash Licker with the stone giant for a boyfriend. The weirdo who carried an amputated doll around with her.

The icy fingers ran cold through every vein in my body. They pinched at every patch of skin, dug in deep, and crawled right through to the bone. I started trembling violently. The tears poured out so hard I could barely see. I wanted to run away, but my legs wouldn't budge. It was like I'd forgotten how to use them.

Madison stopped her clicking and frowned at my tear-soaked face. She tapped her foot rapidly on the step.

"Give it a rest," she snapped. "I haven't sent anything yet."

I couldn't stop crying. Madison groaned in annoyance. She snatched up Hush-a-bye roughly by her hair and flung her in my direction.

The doll skidded across the floor and stopped at my feet. Her unblinking green eyes looked at me. I picked her up, cradled her in my arms, and pressed her hair against my face. No matter how hard I squeezed my eyes shut, the tears kept coming and coming.

"What do you expect?" Madison's voice echoed, like she was shouting from the edge of a distant canyon. "You act like this zombie and never say anything. Never *do* anything.

What do you expect is going to happen? How do you think people are going to treat you?"

"Stop," I whispered into Hush-a-bye's hair through gritted teeth. "Please, stop."

The tapping started up again. "And then you have this weird doll with no arms and legs you've been carrying around for God knows how long. What the heck? Who does that? No wonder everyone calls you Trash Licker."

"Please, please make it stop."

"You know, I wasn't really going to send those pictures. It was only a joke—ha ha, funny, see? But maybe I should. Why not? Let everyone see what a loser you are. It's not my fault. No way. You can't blame me, you're such a freaking disaster."

"Make her stop. Make her stop."

"God! Are you just going to slobber all over that ratty thing? Forget it! I'm sending them now. I can't wait to see—*Ow!*"

Madison's hurt yelp was followed by the bitter smell of something burning. Confused, I peeked through Hush-a-bye's curls.

Madison had one hand clutched in the other, her face grimaced in pain. Her phone lay at her feet. A dark blue flame crackled out of the cracked glass, and a stream of gray smoke rose from it.

I'd never had my own phone, so I thought maybe she'd overloaded it somehow. But there was something in the way the blue flame danced that seemed unnatural. Like something else had put it there. Or *someone*.

"Oh, great," Madison grumbled, rubbing her hand and wincing. "That's just perfect."

A rumbling sound like distant thunder echoed through the room. The sky through the half-open door was dreary and gray, but there was no sign of rain. Still, the rumble went on and on. It didn't die away like thunder usually did. The sound was steady and even, like a huge boulder being rolled away from the entrance to a cave.

I turned to look through one of the high windows in the room, as if the rain might be falling up there for some reason.

That's when I saw it. I had to blink several times to make sure.

Something in my expression made Madison's eyes grow wide. She looked over her shoulder. A horrible, strangled noise caught in her throat. Without taking her eyes off the thing that caught her attention, she started backing down the steps.

That's when I knew for certain I wasn't imagining it. Madison had seen it too.

The Gypsum Man was sitting up in his box.

Madison stumbled on the last step. The giant turned his head, and his empty stone eyes fell upon her. Madison stopped backing away and stared at his stone face.

The Gypsum Man laid his two large hands on the edges of the box. Slowly, like a gathering storm cloud, he lifted himself up to his full height. His head bashed against a low-dangling ceiling light. It shattered and sent down a shower of sparks and glass. The stone man took no notice.

Several shards rained on Madison and startled her out of her daze. With a terrified wail, she twisted about and ran for the half-open door. Just as she reached it, the door slammed shut.

Madison yanked frantically at the doorknob, but the door wouldn't budge. She beat her fists against it.

"Help me! Someone, please!"

All the while, I hadn't moved an inch. Even when the giant lifted his long stone legs over the side of the box and slowly thumped down the steps, I held still.

Not because I was too scared to move, and certainly not because I was brave. But I knew something Madison didn't know. I knew Hush-a-bye had sent the Gypsum Man to help me.

Of all people. *Me.*

I saw the panic and the fear written all over Madison's face as she edged against the wall, desperately trying to find a way out. I drank it all in, and I smiled.

That's right. I actually smiled.

This is what you get Madison, I thought, kissing Hush-a-bye on the top of her head. *This is what you get when you mess with us.*

The Gypsum Man lumbered toward Madison. She screamed and scrambled under a rickety square table, kicking out the chairs at the giant's legs.

The stone man flicked them away like gnats. Madison whimpered. Her face was as drenched with tears as mine had been just a few minutes before.

Now you know, I thought. *Now you know what it's like.*

"I think that's enough, Hush-a-bye," I whispered. "She won't forget this too soon."

The doll said nothing, but I thought I saw a tiny glimmer in her green eyes, like she was winking at me.

I waited for the Gypsum Man to turn back, wondering what I should do next. Should I be gracious and hold out my hand to Madison and let her blubber on my shoulder? Or should I pretend I hadn't seen a thing, and watch her tie herself in knots trying to explain to her friends how a stone giant attacked her. I could imagine the look on their faces.

I started to giggle, but then I stopped. Something wasn't right. The Gypsum Man still hovered over the table where Madison cowered.

"*Fe, fi, fo, fum.*" The Gypsum Man's voice, deep as the ocean, filled the whole room, although his mouth never moved. "*I smell the blood of a nasty one.*"

"She's already had a good scare, Hush-a-bye," I said, puzzled by this strange show the Gypsum Man was putting on. "Let's put him back in his box, okay?"

But the giant didn't back away. Instead, he raised his massive stone fists high above his head.

"*For all the terror and poison she's spread,*" he roared, "*I'll break her bones until she's dead.*"

The stone man thrust his huge fists down at the table. Madison screamed. She dove out from under it a half second before the table crashed and splintered. Shards of wood exploded across the room. The giant's fists smashed into the floor tiles, shattering them.

I stared blankly at the mangled table and broken floor where Madison had been only a moment ago. *Why did he do that?* I thought frantically. *This isn't what I want. He almost killed* her!

A vision of twisted limbs lying in a heap flashed in my mind. My stomach squeezed tight, and I thought I might pass out. Only the sound of Madison screaming brought me to my senses.

The Gypsum Man had Madison backed into a corner. She'd flattened herself against the wall like she was trying to burrow into it. Her eyes were wild, and her usually pink face was now ash-colored. The giant reached out his wide stone hands and grabbed Madison by her waist. She whimpered but didn't try to resist. The fight was all gone from her.

"No," I said, and shook Hush-a-bye. "This is too much."

The Gypsum Man lifted Madison off the ground. Her head lolled to one side. Her eyes were open, but they looked glassy and vacant.

"No more!" I yelled at the doll and shook her harder. "Put her down!"

The stone man raised his arms above his head. Madison's dark hair brushed against the ceiling. He slowly turned about with Madison in his hands lying limp as a rag doll.

"Stop it! Stop it!" I screamed at Hush-a-bye. I screamed until my throat was raw, but it didn't make any difference. And it suddenly dawned on me what was really going on.

Hush-a-bye didn't want to just scare Madison. She wanted to hurt her, to *murder* her. I couldn't let that happen.

I ran up to the stone man and stood in front of him. I cradled Hush-a-bye with one arm and hooked my fingers under her chin.

"Put her down," I said, trying to steady the trembling in my voice. "Put her down right now or I'll tear your head off."

The giant, still holding Madison above his head, looked down at me. There was no sign of life in his stone eyes, but his stare sent shivers through me.

"I'll do it." I pulled up a little on Hush-a-bye's chin. "I'll rip it right off and stomp it into little pieces until there's nothing left." I pulled harder, until there was a cracking noise from the doll's neck.

The Gypsum Man tilted his head to one side like a curious dog. I took a step back, still keeping my fingers hooked under the chin. Sweat ran into my eyes, stinging them. I blinked it away as best as I could.

For what seemed like forever we both stood there, looking at each other, not moving. Then, ever so slowly, the giant lowered his arms and laid Madison out on the floor on her back. She didn't move, but I could hear her breathing.

The stone man strode across the room. I moved back against the wall, never loosening my grip on the doll. The giant climbed the steps, then eased himself back down into his stone coffin. The room went dead silent.

For several seconds I stayed still, my eyes glued to the Gypsum Man's display to see if he had really stopped moving. Slowly, I crept up the steps to edge of his box. The stone man lay in his coffin just like the first time I'd seen him, nothing more than a man-shaped rock.

I drew in a deep breath, then dashed down the steps, shoved Hush-a-bye deep in my bag, and bolted toward the door. It opened without any problem. And I would have shot right out of there, except my way was blocked by Ashley and Gretta and the gang of smirking kids clustered behind them.

There must have been something about the look on my face, because they shrank back from me like I had the plague.

"What is your deal, Trash Licker?" Ashley said, curling up her lips in disgust. "You got rabies or something?"

"Madison," I said breathlessly, pointing back into the room. "She was . . . Help her."

I barreled straight ahead. The crowd jumped away from me, probably wondering if Ashley had a point. I ran as fast as I could, not even bothering to look behind me when Ashley and Gretta started screaming.

17

ONCE I'D LEFT Madison, I'd headed straight for the bus. No other kids were there yet, and the bus driver only glanced up from his newspaper and grunted when he saw me. I bowed my head low and waited.

Not too long after, there were sirens and the flashing lights of an ambulance. A few minutes later, Madison was rolled away on a stretcher while the other kids gawked. Ms. Crozzetti, with her glasses set on top of her head and her arms flailing like a broken windmill, tried to herd the class back on the bus.

Ashley and Gretta spotted me through the bus window. They whispered to Ms. Crozzetti and pointed in my direction. Ms. Crozzetti stared up at me with a look of complete bewilderment.

A streak of lightning cut across the sky, followed by a ripping clap of thunder. And then rain dropped out of the clouds in huge, fat sheets. I moved my bag off the seat and tucked it under my feet as the kids ran onto the bus, soaked to the bone.

Ms. Crozzetti sat next to me the whole ride back, tapping her damp clipboard with a single chipped fingernail. She didn't say a word to me. She didn't even scold the kids when their buzzing chatter grew to a decibel-shattering loudness.

Once we'd returned to school, she ordered the class to brave the downpour and get to their last-period class. Then she took my hand and marched me straight to the principal's office. I barely had time to snatch my bag.

"You can trust me, Laura," Mr. Hendershot said. He wore a fake smile that wouldn't have fooled anybody. "Was there anyone else there with you and Madison Underwood at the Gypsum Man display?"

I barely moved my dripping head from side to side, but it was enough for Mr. Hendershot to consider it a no. My fingers were twisted together tight in my lap. It was the first time I'd ever set foot in the principal's office. It was tinier than I'd imagined, and it smelled like cough drops.

Mr. Hendershot nodded and scratched something on a yellow legal pad. He'd long since given up plying me with any open-ended questions once he'd realized that was going nowhere fast, so he stuck with ones I could answer without words.

That was fine by me. Besides, what could I tell him that he'd ever believe?

Mr. Hendershot's phone rang. He listened, rapping his pencil against the desk, then hung up without saying anything.

"Excuse me, Laura," he said with that same fake smile and left the room, closing the door behind him. Either because it wasn't a very good door or the walls were thin, I heard every word.

"What is it with Laura? Can't she talk?"

"Her name's Lucy," the office secretary said. "She's just shy. I doubt she had anything do with Maddie."

"Who?"

"Madison Underwood. I just received a call from the hospital. She's awake now, and she's claiming she's been assaulted."

"Assaulted by Laura? That scrawny girl? She doesn't look like she could beat up a bag of potato chips."

"It's Lucy. And no, she didn't hurt Maddie. That's the thing. The poor girl is claiming the Gypsum Man attacked her. You know—*the stone statue.*"

Several seconds passed in silence. Then the door opened, and the fake-happy face of Mr. Hendershot poked in.

"You can go back to class now, Laura," Mr. Hendershot said. "Mrs. Bailey will give you a pass."

Twenty minutes later, I was riding the bus home alone. Antonia had another tutoring session that afternoon. I was glad I wouldn't have to explain anything to her right away. A few kids shot me strange looks in passing, but no one said boo to me. I shivered in my still-damp clothes and kept the bag tight on my lap.

When I finally got home, my luck held out. Mom's car wasn't parked by our trailer, so she was still at work. I let myself in and headed straight to the bedroom, closing the door behind me. Without even bothering to take off my wet clothes I dropped the bag, collapsed to the floor, and burst into great big sobs.

After a long, long while, when I'd pretty well emptied myself out, I wiped my face with the back of my sleeve, crawled forward on hands and knees, and, with the last bit of energy I had left, heaved myself onto my bed.

"Ow!"

Something hard dug itself into my ribs. I rolled over and noticed something was under the blanket.

I skittered off the bed and fell back onto Antonia's bed, then kicked off one sneaker and threw it at the lump. It didn't move.

Feeling slightly relieved it wasn't a garter snake that'd found its way into the trailer, I got up and took hold of the top of the blanket. Then I froze. Even before I'd pulled the blanket back, I knew what I'd find under there. But even knowing didn't keep me from shuddering.

I slowly drew back the blanket. And there on my faded, striped bedsheet, laid side by side, were two pale doll's arms.

18

"SHE'S ALMOST WHOLE," I whispered, staring at the doll's arms.

Almost whole. Only Hush-a-bye's legs were missing. And once she had those, then she'd . . .

I blinked. Then she'd what? What would she do when she was finally complete? I had no idea.

The more I thought about it, the more I realized I didn't know anything about this doll. What was she, anyway? A witch? A monster? Or something that didn't even have a name? And what did she want from me and Antonia?

The questions piled up one on top of the other like so many dead leaves, and not one single answer peeked out and hollered from under the whole mess.

Even worse, there was no one I could turn to for help— not Mr. Capp, not May, not even Mom. What would I say? *Excuse me, I think this doll is possessed*? No one would believe me. No one except Antonia.

I bit my lip. *Antonia*. She'd believe me, all right. But I could never tell her what happened with Madison and the Gypsum Man in a million years. Because then I'd have to admit to Antonia why I snuck Hush-a-bye out in the first place. And if I did that, the truth about being the Trash Licker, and all the lies I'd told Antonia to keep her from finding out, would come crashing down on my head. The thought of the pained look on her face once she'd seen who I really was—that scared me more than anything.

I started to feel a little dizzy, so I closed my eyes. *Think, think, think*, I told myself. *What can I do to learn more about Hush-a-bye and figure out what's my next step? Should I search the island again? Or along the riverbank? Maybe do some research in the library—*

My eyes snapped open. "The book!" I'd been so caught up in wondering what evil schemes Madison had planned for me, I'd forgotten about the chapter in the book I'd started reading in the library. The one with the picture of the doll who looked like Hush-a-bye.

I grabbed my backpack and unzipped it. A curl of yellow hair poked out. I jerked back and slammed the back of my legs against the bed. I didn't just forget about the book. I'd forgotten *she* was still in there.

I crept up to the bag and lowered my hands inside until I felt the sides of her body. They felt strangely warm. Like something *alive*. With shaking hands, and with my eyes focused above her head—I didn't want to look into those blank green eyes ever again—I slowly pulled her out of the bag.

The walk to the closet probably took no more than ten seconds, but it felt like hours. Every moment I waited for something horrible to happen, like my hair bursting into flames or a grizzly bear crashing through the trailer walls and eating me. But I managed to get her back on her stand in the closet and quietly close the door without the world ending. I knew a thin door was no protection for what she could do, but at least I didn't have to look at her.

I took a deep breath, pulled out the book from my bag, and sat cross-legged on the floor. Then I thumbed to the article about the young girl and her doll, and I read.

A HUNTER'S MOON LODGE MYSTERY

This is a photograph of Rosetta Hesse, eleven-year-old daughter of the groundskeeper for the Hunter's Moon Lodge, dated October 13, 1878. Two days later, a severe thunderstorm hit Hunter's Moon Island. The hotel was struck with lightning several times. Despite the heavy rain, it quickly burned to the ground. All guests were successfully evacuated, including Rosetta's parents. But Rosetta was not found among the evacuees. She had gone missing. Many assumed the girl had probably drowned.

The morning after the storm, a group of men gathered by the boat dock to undertake a search for

Rosetta. Few had expectations of finding her, until one of them spotted a young girl wandering by the bank of the river. Her hair and dress were completely drenched, but she seemed otherwise unharmed. When questioned about what had happened to her, she claimed to remember nothing. It was assumed she'd suffered a concussion, and she was reunited with her parents.

Several decades later, a local author researching a book about the history of the hotel tracked down Rosetta at a state asylum. Although Rosetta suffered severe memory loss, in a rare moment of lucidity, she related an extraordinary story to the author—she claimed her doll was a demon. These are the author's notes of what Rosetta said:

I've never told anyone what really happened that night when the Hunter's Moon Lodge burned down. I didn't think anyone would believe me. But I need to tell it now while I still can. People need to know the truth.

My story begins a few weeks before the storm hit. At that time, I was the only child living at Hunter's Moon Lodge, and I was very lonely. Loneliness is an awful thing but so much worse when you are young and trying to fill up the endless days.

One day while out walking alone, I heard a voice calling my name. I followed the sound, and eventually I came across a doll sitting in the crook of a tree. I was amazed. But what followed next was even more astounding—the doll began talking to me.

The doll's mouth didn't move, but I could still hear her speak. Maybe it was because I was a child, but I never questioned how such a bizarre thing could be possible. Maybe it was what she said to me. She asked to be my friend. I had been so terribly lonely for so long, I said yes right away. It sounds odd, but at the time it seemed like the most perfectly ordinary thing, and I was thrilled to have a friend to play with, even if it was a doll.

For a time, it was wonderful. I was finally happy. Then strange things began to happen around the hotel. There was a maid who'd scolded me after I'd run into her in the hallway. Later, while she was combing her hair, it began to pull out in huge clumps, leaving her with bald red patches. Then there was a cat that scratched me when I tried to pet him. He was found the next morning mewling wildly, buried up to his neck in an anthill.

When I mentioned these weird occurrences to the doll, she said she had a secret to tell me—she was the one who'd made them happen. I acted like I was surprised, but part of me knew it all along. Still, I asked how it was possible.

She said she was really a magical being from

deep under the river, something like a water sprite. She had lived there for longer than I could imagine, long before the first human walked along the riverside. Where she came from, it was dark and cold and terribly lonely, but when she listened to the voices of the people who began to fill up the land around the river, she found them all to be selfish and cruel and dishonest. She wanted nothing to do with them.

Then one day she heard me talking to myself at the river's edge, and her heart filled with joy. At last she'd found someone who wasn't like the others. Someone like her. Someone who needed a friend. So she rose to the surface and took the form of a doll so I wouldn't be frightened. That's when I found her. And because I was such a wonderful friend to her, she'd made sure anybody who tried to hurt me would think twice before doing it again by using her magic.

"How do you do the magic?" I asked her.

"Through you! Whenever you need my help," she said, "the magic streams out of me and makes those things happen. And every time the magic streams out, a bigger portion of magic streams back into me, and I become stronger and stronger."

"How strong?" I asked. "What could you do?"

"Anything you can imagine. I could split the world in two if I wanted."

I laughed. "But that's impossible."

"Nothing is impossible," she said. "Not any-more."

I didn't know what to make of that, but I didn't let it bother me. Then I asked her one more question. "Can I see what you really look like?"

For a long moment, she was silent. Then she said, "Soon, when the magic is strong enough, I will show you my true face. And then we can be together forever."

I was glad to have such a friend to watch over me, but when I thought of what she'd done to the maid and the cat, and what she meant by being together forever, it unsettled me. But I tried not to think about it too much. Then came the storm, and everything changed.

That night, I was on the first floor of the hotel with the doll when the fire bells sounded. I'd heard the loud thunder crack and smelled the stench of burning, and I wondered aloud if there might be a fire in the hotel. Suddenly, the doll frantically screamed at me to get her away from the building. I was startled by the fearful tone in her voice, one I'd never heard before. I ran out into the storm and over to the docks to be as far from the fire as possible. Even then, she demanded—that's the word for it: demanded—I take a boat out in the river to get her even farther away.

As I rowed out in the middle of the swirling waters, she began muttering about the persons living in the hotel who were out to destroy her. I tried to explain the lightning was probably the source of the fire, but she wouldn't listen. And then she laid out the things she would do to get her revenge on all of them, her voice dripping with anger and malice.

The terrible, cruel things she said she would do to each of them—I can't even repeat them. It still makes me sick when I think about it. And it was at that moment I knew she was no water sprite. She was surely a demon from hell, and when she grew strong enough and laid waste to everything, she'd drag me back down with her to the fiery pits. I knew what I had to do.

I moved so quickly she had no time to react. First I tore off her head and threw it in the river. Then I did the same with her arms and her legs, and then finally her body. I threw them all in different directions and watched them sink.

I don't know how long I sat in that boat. It broke my heart to lose the only friend I'd made on the island, but I have no regrets. The world is a better place without that doll in it, and I hope she remains at the bottom of that river until the end of time.

Rosetta died two weeks later after speaking with the author. No part of her strange story has

ever been corroborated, and because she was often
delusional—

The front door of the trailer creaked open. I slammed the
book closed and whipped my head around, half expecting
Hush-a-bye's limbless body to be floating there like some de-
mented ghost. Nothing was there.

I rapped my knuckle on my forehead a couple of times,
scolding myself for being such a wimp. I grabbed the doll's
arms and shoved them and the book under my bed. When
Antonia opened our bedroom door, I squeezed past, shouting "Taking a shower" before she had a chance to say anything.

I stayed under the shower until I was shriveled as an old
raisin. Mom would have killed me for wasting so much water, but that didn't seem like the biggest thing in the world to
worry about right then. I had to think this through without
any distractions.

I didn't have any doubt that Rosetta's doll and Hush-a-
bye were the same. There were a whole lot of things about her
story that were scarily familiar, especially the part about how
the doll enjoyed causing pain. On the other hand, I really
didn't have a better idea of what Hush-a-bye was than before.
Rosetta called her a demon from hell, but I never believed in
a place like that. People might be mean and judgy, but I figured God, if there was one, would be better than that. And
though Rosetta had taken Hush-a-bye apart and dumped her

in the river, it was pretty clear it hadn't put an end to her.

After a while, it seemed the more I thought about it, the less I understood what was going on. So I shut off the water and got out of the shower.

When I came back, the bedroom was quiet and empty, which was a relief. I sat cross-legged on my bed and started drying my hair with a towel. The closet door opened.

Antonia came out, frowning. She closed the door and leaned back against it.

"I don't get it," she said, fidgeting with her sparkly duckling barrette.

"Don't get what?" I pretended like the only thing that mattered was how dry I could get my hair.

Antonia looked at me like she hadn't realized I was in the room. She stared at me, turned toward the closet, and turned back again. It had been so many days since we'd had a real conversation together, it was like she'd forgotten how.

"Hush-a-bye," she said finally.

"Oh? What about her?" I rubbed my hair so frantically I thought it might catch fire.

"The sash around her dress is gone. But she won't tell me why. She won't even talk to me."

I stopped rubbing. Hush-a-bye not talking wasn't what I expected, but it wasn't unwelcome news. "I wouldn't worry about it too much. You can still talk to me."

Antonia kicked backward at the door, so hard I thought it might splinter. "But she always talks to me. She always listens to me. I can't even tell if she's listening."

"Maybe she doesn't feel like talking today." I tossed the towel to the end of my bed. "Like I said, I'm still here. You can talk to me. If you want to."

Antonia stared at me. It was such a hard stare my skin felt prickly.

"What?" I asked.

"Did you do something to her?"

Now I was really feeling prickly. I hoped my face didn't look as red as it felt. "Of course I didn't do anything to her. Why would you say that?"

"The last thing Hush-a-bye said to me before I left her in the closet was 'Watch out for Lucy.' I didn't know what she meant, but now I'm wondering."

Watch out for Lucy. I shivered. How would Hush-a-bye have known I was going to take her on the field trip? Still, I made a big show of rolling my eyes and groaning. "Well, of course you should watch out for me. Just like I watch for you. We watch out for each other. That's what sisters are supposed to do, aren't they?"

She frowned, but I could tell she was trying to figure out if what I said made sense. When the frown softened and she looked at me with shining eyes, I knew I'd convinced her.

"You don't think some river witch might have stolen her sash, do you? Like maybe that's where she kept all her magic?" she asked in a pitiful voice. I had to bite the inside of my cheek to keep from crying myself. "Maybe she blames me for not keeping her magic safe. Maybe she's thinking about leaving me!"

If only, I thought. "I don't think so," I said. "She had magic before you found the sash, remember? I bet she just wanted to loosen up her clothes, so she poofed it away. You know she could do it."

Antonia nodded, frowning again. "I guess. Still doesn't explain why she's giving me the silent treatment."

"All that extra magic probably tired her out. She's resting, that's all. Just give her some time. Hey, you want to check out the ginkgo tree? I thought I saw a leaf falling down when I came home."

It was a lie, but I figured one more wouldn't make any difference. She screwed up her face for a bit thinking it over, but after a few more glances over her shoulder, she nodded feebly and followed me out.

Of course when we got outside, using the kitchen garbage lid as our umbrella, the leaves hadn't come down, even with the downpour. Not a single one. But it felt good to be doing something with Antonia again, even if she was a little sulky. It had been too long.

When I'd returned to school the next day, my role in the whole episode of Madison and the Gypsum Man was pretty well forgotten. All anyone could talk about was how Madison, so perfect and so put together, had dived off the deep end.

Rumors about what caused it flew everywhere. Some said the strain of being an A++ student finally got to her, and some whispered about weird drugs. All anyone agreed on was she must have hallucinated her attack by the stone statue. Or, as her supposed best friend Ashley Oslo so nicely put it, "I think her brain overheated and melted. That's a real thing that can happen, isn't it?"

It was all the twins gossiped about in the hallways. Without Madison to egg them on, they ignored me completely. After all, what was one mousy girl compared to a popular honor student losing it?

You'd think it would've been a relief to me to have Madison out of the picture and not catching any flak for the whole mess. But I couldn't shake the look of fear I'd seen on Madison's face, and the cold light in Hush-a-bye's eyes. Awful as Madison had been to me, I never wanted to hurt her. Not like that.

But Hush-a-bye did. And I wondered, now that I'd threatened her, if she'd do the same to me. Each night when I tried to sleep, those horrible green eyes would flash before me. I'd bolt upright, panting and sweating.

Sometimes I imagined myself throwing her back in the river like Rosetta just to get her out of the way. But I also imagined her dragging me with her down to the muddy bottom. *Nothing is impossible. Not anymore.*

After the second sleepless night, I was sitting in Mr.

Capp's regular art class with the dog book open in front of me. My eyelids felt like they weighed about a hundred pounds each. My fingers could barely hold on to the pencil. The picture of the Doberman I was supposed to be drawing grew hazy and melted away.

A clattering sound made me jerk my head up. I looked to my side and saw my pencil had dropped to the floor. I blinked my eyes rapidly, trying to get rid of the fog in my brain.

Before I could bend down to retrieve the pencil, Mr. Capp was holding it and offering it back to me. His face wore a concerned smile. Unlike the principal's smile, though, there was nothing fake about it.

"You feeling okay, Lucy?" he asked as I took back the pencil. I gave a quick nod.

He glanced out the window and sighed. "Must be this weather. It's enough to put anyone off." The rain beat against the pane loudly, and the sky was the color of wet clay.

Ever since that thunderclap at the Old Hops Village, the rain hadn't let up for a moment. The weatherman on the TV called it "the storm of the century." There was already flooding in some of the lowlands close to the river. Our trailer rested on a rise several feet above where the river would crest if it did flood, but Mom, exhausted as she was, still fretted over the weather report each night.

"Why don't you put that away for now," Mr. Capp said, gently closing the book. "There's time enough for that some other day. If you want to lay your head down and rest for a bit, I'll pretend not to notice."

He winked and walked away. I didn't put my head down, but I was grateful for the offer.

By Thursday night, I was so worn-out that Madison's face and Hush-a-bye's eyes and Antonia's buffalo snoring couldn't stop my eyelids from closing. I finally fell asleep—and landed right in a nightmare.

19

IN MY DREAM, I stood on the bank of the Susquehanna, looking out toward the island. The morning sun was headache-bright in a cloudless sky, and the birch trees on the island glimmered.

My feet were bare, and my toes were poking into the brown-green water. It felt so cool and inviting, I thought I'd wade right in. But the moment I put my foot forward, I found myself already standing on the grassy slope of the island.

The birch trees above the slope were gone. I spotted a gravel path off to one side leading up from the river's edge, and I followed the path until I came to a long white two-story building—the Hunter's Moon Lodge I'd read about. It was in the same spot where I'd seen those charred pine posts when Antonia and I had come over in the boat to find Hush-a-bye's body. Tinny, old-time piano music and a jumble of voices and laughter drifted toward me from inside the lodge.

I searched around for a door but couldn't find one. So I

took a step forward to get a closer peek through one of the windows. Before I even set my foot down, I was already inside the building.

It looked like the lobby of one of those hotels from a hundred years ago you see in movies about rich people. The carpet, dark red and an inch deep, led up to a mahogany front desk, while off to the side was a winding staircase with shiny, carved railings. A crystal chandelier glittered above my head as white sunlight streamed through a wide, clear window. Big stacks of luggage were piled up at the front desk.

No one was there. The music and the voices had stopped. I crept forward and stood on my tiptoes to ring the bell on the front desk. It tinged loudly, and the echo fluttered all around the room.

I waited. No one came.

A shuffling sound from the top of the stairs caught my attention. I climbed the staircase to investigate. At the top, a long hallway extended off to the right, lit with rows of old-fashioned gas lamps.

Somewhere at the far end of the hallway, the shuffling sound started again, then abruptly stopped.

"Hello?" I said. No answer. I hesitated, then entered the hall.

As I crept along, I turned the door handles of each room I passed. All were locked. Sometimes I heard whispering behind the doors. When I pressed my ear against one, the whispering stopped. Then, from somewhere far away—I couldn't tell where—I heard a voice singing.

> *Hush-a-bye and good night*
> *Till the bright morning light*
> *Takes the sleep from your eyes*
> *Hush-a-bye, baby bright*

The last room at the end of the hallway was prettied up with a pair of white French doors with frosted glass panels. I couldn't see anything through the panels, but I knew someone in there was waiting for me. I reached out my hand, but the doors swung open all on their own with a faint, silky hush. I stepped inside.

The room was bare and colorless, with a shiny parquet floor and a large bay window at one end. But it wasn't empty. A thin girl knelt in the center with her back to me. She had long, curly blond hair and wore a dress like Hush-a-bye's with frills at the arms and the bottom. And just like Hush-a-bye's dress, the sash was missing.

"She's hungry," the girl said in voice that seemed to echo out of a deep pit. I walked to her, and she turned her head.

I drew back a little. Her face was covered with a mask— all white except for two red dots for cheeks and small red butterfly lips. Some kind of thick gauze covered the eyeholes.

The French doors clicked shut behind me. I whipped

about and yanked at the handles, but the doors wouldn't budge.

"You shouldn't have kept me waiting so long," the masked girl said.

"I can't get out," I said between gulps of breath.

"Never mind about that. First things first. You know what to do."

"What to do?"

The masked girl clamped cold hands on my shoulders and spun me a quarter turn. I saw a massive iron door built into the wall. I wondered how I hadn't noticed it before. It was crusted over with gray fish bones and thick vines.

The girl shoved me hard toward the door. I slammed into it, then dropped to the floor with a whimper and drew my knees up to my chest. A shower of bones and dead leaves fell all around me.

"Open the door," she said.

"I can't . . . I can't," I pleaded.

"You will," she hissed. "Think you can back out now after letting that nasty girl steal my sash and not expect to pay? Think you're something special? You're nothing without me."

"I don't want to do this anymore," I whispered.

"Too late." Something cold and damp swept over my feet. I stood up quickly. Rust-colored water leaked from the bottom and sides of the iron door. A crash of waves boomed from the other side.

"Open the door," the masked girl commanded.

I shook my head. "I want to wake up now."

The masked girl laughed. "You think this is a dream? You think you can escape by opening your eyes?" She came closer. I tried to move off to the side, but something held my feet in place. I couldn't move.

"It's all real, Lucy," the masked girl said in a familiar voice, like someone trying to talk through a mouthful of mud. "This hotel. This room. What's waiting for you on the other side of the door. And me. We're all as real as the bed you're sleeping on right now. And there's no one you can tell who'll believe you. You're all alone. Poor Lucy. All alone like you'll always be."

"I want it to end," I said, sobbing.

"It will. Very soon. It's all going to end. But first I want to show you something. I want to show you my real face."

She gripped her mask with one hand and with the other undid the string at the back of her head.

Outside the bay window, a slash of lightning cut across the sky. I clutched my hands to my chest while the freezing water rose up around my ankles, and then to my knees, to my hips, and to my shoulders.

"Good night, Lucy, sleep tight," the girl said.

And then she took off her mask.

20

I OPENED MY eyes in the darkness of my bedroom and clamped both hands over my mouth to hold back the scream.

For several minutes, I lay there in my bed, shaking as if my mattress were a huge block of ice. I hardly dared to blink.

It's all going to end. The words played over and over in my mind as the rain drummed down on the aluminum roof of our trailer. I didn't want to imagine what she meant.

It was all too, too much. Why was this happening? What did I ever do to ask for this?

I bit my bottom lip. The answer to that was obvious.

I asked for Hush-a-bye's help.

I thought back to the beginning of the year and how the scariest thing in my life was getting through seventh grade. It seemed like such a small thing now. What I wouldn't have given to go back in a time machine to that day by the river. I'd warn myself to not kick away the willow branch or pick up that doll's head. I still would have been just as miserable and friendless, but at least I'd be the only one who got hurt.

But I couldn't go back. No sense in even thinking about it. And I couldn't hide my head in the sand and pretend it would all blow over. This time, the Rules wouldn't work.

I had to do something. For me. For Antonia. Even for Madison. I couldn't let someone else tell me how my story was going to end.

I flipped out my legs and crept across the room to the closet. I pressed my ear against the door and listened. Antonia was still snoring loudly on her bed, but no sound came from inside the closet.

I turned the knob and opened the closet door as quietly as possible. My hands trembled. I felt about in the dark space until my fingers brushed against lacy fabric. Swallowing hard, I wrapped my fingers around the dress and pulled out Hush-a-bye.

Her green eyes glinted in the darkness. I quickly placed my hand over them and closed the door. Then I grabbed the doll arms from under my bed and carried all of Hush-a-bye out of the bedroom.

In the kitchen, I wrapped the doll parts in a trash bag, then put on my cheap plastic poncho and snuck outside in my bare feet.

The rain beat down just as hard as ever, as if every bit of water from every part of world had decided to flow to Oneega Valley that night. With every step I had to yank my feet out of cold, slimy mud. It was slow going.

With every step, I expected tree branches to reach out and grab me, or a wave of mud to rise up and bury me alive. I'd seen what Hush-a-bye could do. There was no way I could stop her if she put her mind to it.

None of that kept me from doing what I knew had to be done. I was betting Hush-a-bye wouldn't harm me or Antonia. We were the ones who'd rescued her, after all. She owed us that much, I figured. At least, that's what I kept telling myself as I sloshed around to the back of the trailer.

I finally made it to the trash can. I moved aside some empty frozen corn bags and pushed Hush-a-bye deep into the can.

"I'm sorry," I said as I covered her with the bags and set the lid back. "Don't blame Antonia. This is all my idea."

I wondered if she knew I was going to throw her into the river the next day after school. I knew it wouldn't destroy her, but it had taken her over a hundred years to claw her way back the last time. Another hundred years sunk in the river mud was good enough for now.

I'd have done it that night, but I could barely find my way to the rear of our trailer through all that black rain. At least it would be lighter tomorrow, even if it was still raining. I'd find a plastic grocery bag to stuff her in so I wouldn't have to look at those scary green eyes and pale arms and—

I froze with my hand still on the lid. *The sash.* Hush-a-bye's shiny red sash. I'd almost forgotten. Madison had stolen it and put it in her pocket before the stone giant had attacked her. The girl in the dream had remembered it being stolen from her. Madison still had a piece of Hush-a-bye.

Maybe it was nothing more than a plain old red ribbon, but I couldn't take anything for granted. No, I had to get that sash back and throw it in the water with the rest of Hush-a-bye. I wanted every part of that doll deep underwater. I wasn't taking any chances.

But that meant I'd have to get it back from Madison. Icy fingers drummed on my head when I considered it, and it wasn't just the rain.

It was going to be the hardest thing I'd ever done in my life. Harder than getting on the bus in the morning with the whole awful day ahead of me, harder even than facing down some demon doll from hell. Nothing else even came close.

I was going to have to break every single one of the Rules.

21

"SHE'S GONE!"

Antonia burst out of our bedroom closet in a wild-eyed panic. I was still rubbing sleepiness and morning crud from my eyes.

I pulled my feet out from under my blanket and was puzzled for a moment by my mud-caked toes. But then the *rat-a-tat* of the rain on the trailer roof jogged my memory. *Right. Hush-a-bye. Make an excuse.*

"Shh," I said, and waved Antonia over to me. "Not so loud. I have to tell you something about Hush-a-bye."

Antonia bounced over her bed and slammed next to me. "What? What?"

"I overheard Mom talking to a friend on the phone last night," I whispered. "She said she was going to clean out our closet before she went to work, so I hid Hush-a-bye in my bottom drawer."

Antonia let out a long breath and fell backward on the

bed. "Thank goodness," she said. "I thought she'd run away for good. You know she hasn't said a word to me all week."

"I know," I said. "Give her time."

"Time? Time for what?" Antonia pulled on my arm. "Do you know something, Lucy? Did she tell you something about me? Did I do something wrong?" She dug her nails hard into my arm. Her eyes were wild. "Tell her I didn't mean it, whatever it was. I didn't mean it!"

I yanked Antonia's fingers out and pushed her away. "Stop it, Antonia. You didn't do anything. And no, she didn't talk to me. Sometimes dolls don't feel like talking."

I felt lower than a worm lying to my sister so much. But I didn't have a choice. I still had to take care of too many things, and it would be too hard to try and explain it all, especially about Hush-a-bye. When it was all finished, with Hush-a-bye sunk to the bottom of the river, I promised myself I'd come clean with Antonia. She might hate me at first, but she'd get over it. Eventually.

"Can I at least say goodbye to Hush-a-bye before I go to school?" Antonia asked, biting her fingers. "I don't want her to think I forgot her."

"Okay," I said. "I've tucked her under some sweaters, so you can't take her out. Mom might walk in. Just say goodbye through the closed drawer."

Antonia said her goodbyes in a half-choked voice and kissed the drawer knobs for good measure. Once we got on the bus, she was so distracted with thoughts about that horrible doll she started lifting her hand to wave at Gus when he walked down the bus aisle offering her a shy half smile. But partway up she remembered she was still supposed to be mad at him and quickly dropped her hand back down. Her red cheeks told another story.

I couldn't let myself focus on that drama. I was too busy rehearsing for Mr. Capp. *Mr. Capp, can I ask you a question? Excuse me, Mr. Capp? Would it be all right if I asked you a quick question? Pardon me, Mr. Capp, but do you have a minute to answer a question?*

None of it sounded right. At least, coming out of my mouth it didn't. I'd already tried a hundred different variations all morning before the bus pulled up. It wasn't getting any better.

Once I got off the bus, I marched past my homeroom and headed straight for Mr. Capp's art room. *Here we go*, I thought, and I walked through the door.

Mr. Capp was erasing the whiteboard with his back to me. I took a step toward him, and my legs instantly turned to jelly. *I'm not ready for this. Maybe next week would be better.*

I grabbed my bag and made for the door, and then I stopped myself.

No. Today. I spun about and faced Mr. Capp once more.

I opened my mouth, then shut it. *Forget it*, I thought. *He should have been looking at me. Some other time when he's facing the right way.* I took a short backward step, then stopped again.

No, no, no. No more excuses. Stop being ridiculous. I clutched my bag tight in my hand and cleared my throat.

"M-Mr. Capp?" I stuttered.

Mr. Capp looked over his shoulder. He stared across the room with a puzzled look, like he couldn't figure out who'd spoken to him, even though I was the only one standing there.

"Mr. Capp?" I said again, not feeling any better about it than the first time. "Can . . . can I ask you something?"

Mr. Capp's mouth dropped open a smidge. For one brief, horrible second, I pictured him hoisting me up on his shoulders and parading me about the school while I performed my miraculous talking trick. But he only smoothed the sides of his mustache with one hand and smiled.

"Of course, Lucy," he said. "You can and you may ask me anything at all."

I took a breath. "Do you know Madison? I mean Maddie Underwood? She's a seventh grader like me."

Mr. Capp scratched his chin thoughtfully. "Second period. Yes, I know her. Smart girl. Good color sense. Why do you ask?"

"I was . . . I've been worried about her since she's not been in school the last few days and I thought maybe you had some work for her I could take to her house if that's okay please thank you." I gulped after saying all those words in one breath, not really sure if I was making any sense.

Mr. Capp looked at me for a while without saying

anything. I wondered if he was considering calling the police on the lunatic girl talking nonsense in his classroom. But then he folded his arms and smiled.

"Well, I don't really do homework, as you know, but I suppose I could throw something together to keep her busy," he said. "Do you have a way of getting to her house?"

I swallowed hard. "Getting to her house?"

"Yes. Can you get to Maddie's house after school?"

"Oh . . . yes. Yes, I can. She's on my bus route. So . . . yes. And I can walk home from there."

Mr. Capp smiled. "Perfect." He opened his desk drawer and pulled out a brown compact umbrella. "First, take this."

I stared at the umbrella but didn't move.

"It's all right, you can have it," he said, motioning me to come closer. "I bought myself a new one last week, and I've been meaning to rid of this one. There's nothing wrong with it—except for being god-awful ugly."

I giggled and took the umbrella.

"Tell you what. I'll also call the office to see if they have any other teachers' homework lying about. I'll tell them you've volunteered to take it all to Maddie's home," Mr. Capp said. "Does that work for you?"

"Uh, sure," I said, nodding my head like an eager cocker spaniel.

Mr. Capp clapped his hands together and smiled again. "Good! Make sure you stop by the office before you leave today. Right now you better hurry on to your homeroom." Mr.

Capp sat down and leaned back in his chair, folding his hands behind his head.

I nodded again, thinking I'd already used up all my words, but a few more I hadn't planned to say suddenly popped into my head. I wasn't really sure how to get them out unprompted, so I cleared my throat again.

Mr. Capp propped his neon green sneakers on his desk. "Was there something else?"

"Yes." I took a deep breath. "Would . . . would it be okay if I drew something else besides dogs?"

He smiled so big his mustache almost banged against his eyeballs. "You may draw whatever your dear heart desires. We'll talk more about exactly what that might be during art class, okay?"

"Okay. Thanks."

"Of course. And thank *you*, Lucy."

I left the art room with my heart racing a million miles a minute. I felt like I'd run a marathon and had finally crossed the finish line.

It was exhausting. But it felt good.

Then again, it was easy being with Mr. Capp. He said all the right things, didn't prod me when I was silent, and never once asked me why I'd started talking to him in the first place.

I knew the good feeling wouldn't last long. I may have succeeded with the first part of my plan, but the second part was going to be a thousand times harder.

I was going to have to ask Madison to return the red sash she'd stolen.

Madison. Who thought I was garbage. Who'd rather see me covered in honey and dropped headfirst into a hill of fire ants than talk to me. That Madison.

But I knew I had to do it anyway, and not just because of the sash. I had to make sure she was okay.

Nasty as she was, she didn't deserve to be hurt so badly. No one deserved that. And it was my fault it happened in the first place. After all, it was me who'd brought that demon doll on the field trip, begging her to stop Madison from tearing me down. And even before that, it was me who'd told Antonia we could bring the doll's head home.

I remembered what the masked girl in the dream had said to me. *There's no one you can tell who'll believe you. You're all alone.* It stung me because it was true. I imagined Madison must be feeling the same way. I wouldn't wish that on anyone. Not even Madison.

I had to make things right, or at least I had to try. That was the plan, anyway. It was a horrible plan, for sure, but it was the only plan I had.

22

"HERE WE ARE," the bus driver said. "Two houses down on your right. The big yellow house. You can't miss it."

I stepped off the bus and opened the umbrella, silently thanking Mr. Capp for the gift. The rain was coming down so hard I probably would have drowned before I made it past the first house.

The downpour was hard to see through, but I could still tell this neighborhood was nothing like mine. These people had money. I felt like the windows of every house looked down on me, whispering nasty comments about my dirty sneakers and cheap clothes. Even the sidewalks looked more expensive than the cracked slabs near the trailer park.

It was worse when I opened the gate to Madison's house—except it wasn't really a house. It was a mansion, like something out of the movies. Tall Greek columns, neatly trimmed hedges, and an expensive-looking car waiting in the long driveway to take Madison and her family places I wasn't welcome. The plan was already crumbling in my brain.

My shoulders slumped, and I plodded my way to the front door. Despite the heavy rain, I stood for several minutes on the stoop, waiting for lightning to strike me. It didn't, so I rang the doorbell. The door opened almost immediately. I pulled the umbrella down over my face.

"Oh my, come in, come in," a man's voice said on the other side of the umbrella. "Lord love a duck, look at all that rain!"

I closed up the umbrella while I was still outside, forgetting about the downpour, and I was instantly drenched. A large hand took hold of my elbow and led me in.

"My word, you'll catch your death of cold standing out there," the man's voice said. He spoke with a slow drawl, and it gave his words a strange and wonderful kind of music. I wiped the rain out of my eyes and stared.

The man had a close-trimmed gray beard, and he wore a dark blue suit. His eyes were light amber, bright and warm. He smiled at me—a Mr. Capp kind of smile.

"I'm guessing you must be Lucy Bloom," the man said as he shook out my umbrella. "I'm Dr. Underwood, Maddie's dad. The school office called and told me you'd be coming over with her homework. As luck would have it, my root canal canceled this afternoon, so I was able to get home in time to let you in."

I handed over the now-soggy homework folder. Dr. Underwood held it by a corner. He pursed his lips as it dripped, then set it on a marble side table. "I'm sure it'll dry out in no time. That was awful kind of you to bring it, especially on such a nasty day. Can I get you a towel? How about some cocoa?"

I shook my head. "I'm fine, thank you. Would . . . would it be okay if I talked to Madison, uh, Maddie?"

Dr. Underwood stroked his beard and nodded. "I get it. You're worried about her. It's been a hard week for all of us with Maddie's, um, condition, and my wife up half the night with the baby."

"The baby?" I had no idea Madison had a new sibling. She'd never mentioned it to either one of the Oslo twins during those times she wasn't talking about me.

"Oh yeah," Dr. Underwood said. "Little bugger's had a bad case of colic lately. We've tried walking him and rubbing his back and a whole bunch of other things. None of it seems to do any good." He sighed and shook his head, then laughed. "But here I am yapping away about my problems. Let me take you on up to Maddie's room. I'm sure she'd be happy as a clam to see a friendly face from school."

Dr. Underwood led me up a staircase with a banister that looked too polished to touch. I hoped he couldn't hear the rumbling in my stomach or the blood pounding in my ears. He'd been so pleasant—so un-Madison-like. It was obvious he had no idea his daughter might not exactly consider me a "friendly face."

For all I knew, she might take one look at me and start screaming for her father to boot out the Trash Licker who'd nearly killed her. Or maybe she'd just point at me and laugh while I stood there like a statue and took it. Or worse yet—what if Ashley and Gretta were already in there, ready to gang up on me?

We reached the landing, and my mind raced. *What am I doing here? What do I hope to accomplish?* I hadn't given any thought to what I might say like I had with Mr. Capp. With every step, I grew more and more certain this plan to get the sash was doomed to failure. Everyone would be better off if I ran away and forgot all about it.

But before I knew it, we were standing in front of Madison's bedroom door. Dr. Underwood laid a gentle hand on my shoulder.

"I'll be back in about ten minutes," he said in a low voice. "I don't want to overdo it right now. She's doing better, but the first couple of days after her . . . collapse . . . were pretty hard."

I nodded, digging my nails in my palm. Dr. Underwood smiled and opened the door.

If the house was like something out of the movies, Madison's room was like something you'd see in a teen fashion magazine. Pastel curtains and matching wallpaper, a glass desk with an enormous laptop, another table with a wide mirror and enough product to open a salon, a flat-screen TV hung from the wall like a picture frame, and an enormous frilly bed with more pillows and plush cats than any three people might need.

In the middle of the bed lay Madison, shooting me a stare that would have frozen Mount Vesuvius.

"Maddie-kins?" Dr. Underwood said. "Look who's come out to visit you on such a rainy day." Dr. Underwood stood there looking back and forth between me and Madison. Neither of us said a word.

"Okay, then," Dr. Underwood said with a chuckle. "You can't have any of your girl talk with an old man like me puttering around. Lucy won't be able to stay for too long, though, Maddie. I'll be back to shoo her out in a few minutes."

He smiled again, completely unaware of the arctic frost covering every inch of the room, and closed the door.

The silence stretched between me and Madison. She wore no makeup, and her hair looked a little squashed against her head, like she'd just woke up. All she wore were sweatpants and an oversized sweatshirt.

I'd never seen her so un-put together. She looked smaller somehow, like she'd shed a skin or two. Then again, even like that, she was still prettier than I could ever hope to be.

At the same time, seeing her looking so alone in her huge bed, like a raft adrift in the ocean, my nervousness dissolved a little bit. She didn't seem as scary as she used to—she was just another girl.

I took a step toward the bed. Madison stiffened, so I stopped.

I still didn't know what to say to her, any more than I knew if she planning to leap off the bed at any moment and scratch my eyes out, but I decided to start talking anyway. I hoped either something would come to me, or at the very least she wouldn't go for the eyes first. "I like your room," I said. "It's bigger than the one me and Antonia share."

"Antonia?" Madison mumbled.

"My little sister. She sits with me on the bus."

Madison nodded, but I couldn't tell if she was listening. Her eyes darted all over the room, looking everywhere except at me. I plowed ahead anyway.

"Your dad said you have a little baby brother now."

"Thomas." Madison frowned at the name. "He's always crying."

While I was talking I'd been inching closer to the bed without really thinking about it. Madison didn't seem to notice or care. She just twirled a strand of hair around her finger while her eyes buzzed about the room. But then I tripped over a shoe and stumbled against the bed.

Madison gave a little shriek and shrank back. "What are you doing here? What do you want?" she asked, like she'd suddenly noticed I was in her room. She pulled the comforter tight against her body. I stepped back, a little stunned. Then I took in a breath and let it out slow.

"I need the red sash you took," I said. "The one tied around the doll's dress. It's important to me."

Madison stared at me like I was speaking gibberish, and then understanding slowly crept into her eyes and she blushed.

"Oh, right." She let go of the comforter and slid off the far side of the bed. I'd been worried she might deny she'd taken it in the first place, but I supposed all the fight had been drained out of her, at least for the moment. At her dresser, she opened a jewelry box studded with what looked like gumdrops and pulled out the sash, holding it gingerly between her thumb and finger like it was a worm.

She walked over to me, doing her best not to look me in the eyes, and dropped it in my open palm. "I don't know why I took it." She quickly scuttled away back to the center of her bed. "I'm . . . I'm . . ."

Sorry *is the word you're searching for,* I thought to myself, but bit my tongue. "It doesn't matter," I said, poking the sash in my pocket. "Thanks."

"Sure." Madison chewed on her bottom lip. "Is that the only reason you're here? For the sash?"

"Well, no," I told her. "I wanted to see if you're doing okay."

"Oh." Madison snatched a tissue from an end table and dabbed her red-rimmed eyes. "What are they saying about me?" she asked. "Did Ashley and Gretta say anything about me?" She stared down at the crumpled tissue in her hand and sniffed. "They all think I've lost it."

It sounded like Ashley and Gretta hadn't visited her since the field trip. Probably no one had. No one but the Trash Licker.

This should have been my big moment, the part where I'd

point out how pathetic and friendless she was, where I'd rub her misery in her face and say *See how you like it*.

But the spite was all burned to ashes in me. The loneliness in her voice hit me hard, because I knew how it felt. *There's no one you can tell who'll believe you. You're all alone.* Sure, she'd been nothing but vicious to me ever since I'd known her, but I figured my almost getting her killed and her friends thinking she'd had some kind of breakdown evened things out more or less. So instead, I said what I thought was the one thing Madison needed to hear the most.

"I was there with you, Madison, remember?" I said. "I was there with you and the Gypsum Man. I saw what he did to you. I saw it all."

Madison lifted her head and stared at me, her eyes glistening. She opened her mouth to say something, when the door opened.

"Sorry, girls," Dr. Underwood said. "Time's up. But don't worry, Maddie-kins. You'll be seeing her back at school before you know it."

Madison turned away to grab another tissue. "Okay," she said in a choked voice.

I couldn't think of anything else to add, so I walked toward the door. Then Madison spoke and I stopped.

"Bye," she said, then added, "Lucy." She faced me again, and the barest of smiles crossed her lips.

I grinned and paid back the smile double. "Bye, Maddie."

23

DR. UNDERWOOD INSISTED on driving me home. The endless rain pounded against his beautiful car all the way back to the trailer. I didn't care. I was too happy to care.

I'd broken the Rules with Mr. Capp and Dr. Underwood, and even with Maddie. Somehow, the world hadn't cracked in half, a stray lightning bolt hadn't zapped me into a black smudge, and God knows what else I thought was going to happen. I was still all in one piece.

I remembered Hush-a-bye was lying in the garbage can, waiting to be thrown in the river. The funny thing was, it didn't seem like such a big deal anymore. What did one spooky, mixed-up doll matter? I'd talked to people, including my worst enemy in the world, and they'd talked back. Nothing was impossible for me. Not anymore.

I thanked Dr. Underwood as he dropped me off at the side of the road near the trailer. The rain gushed down like all the cloud spigots had been broken wide open. I didn't care about that either.

I closed up the umbrella and let the rain soak me. I stomped my way home and squished my sneakers through the chain of puddles covering the ground, making sure I didn't miss a single one.

I'd already decided to waste no time and take care of Hush-a-bye immediately, rain or no rain. I'd dump her sorry little doll butt in the river, and then I'd break the news to Antonia.

No more lies, though. I'd tell her everything—about the Rosetta story, the strange dream I'd had, the way the Gypsum Man nearly killed Maddie, and why I decided to bury Hush-a-bye in the muddy Susquehanna. Antonia might not like it at first, but she'd come around in the end. After all, we were sisters. Nothing could come between us for too long.

As I drew closer to the trailer, I just barely made out the ginkgo tree through the heavy sheet of rain. I couldn't believe it. In spite of the wind and the constant hammer of the downpour, all its leaves still hung on.

"Good for you," I said. I blew a kiss to the tree and laughed. Then I spotted Mom's car parked alongside the tree, and my laughter cut off as quickly as it started.

It didn't make sense. Mom was scheduled to work late that night. She shouldn't have been home for another five hours. Something was wrong.

I ran the rest of the way to the trailer and banged open the door. Mom stood by the couch with the phone in her hand. Her eyes looked wild, and when she saw me, she froze.

"Mom?" I said.

Mom slammed down the phone, rushed over, and grabbed me hard by the arms.

"Where the hell were you?" she shouted in my face, her fingernails digging painfully into my skin.

I stood there, stunned, my heart banging against my ribs.

"I—I was with a friend," I stammered out. My eyes grew hot with tears.

"A friend," Mom repeated. The wild look drained from her eyes, and her bottom lip trembled. She pulled me into a tight hug and buried her face in my neck.

"Mom?" Her hug scared me more than the shaking. "Is something wrong?"

Mom pulled back and wiped her face with the back of her hand. She forced a smile. "I—I'm so sorry, Peppernose. You gave me such a scare when I came home and you weren't here."

"Why are you home so early? Did something happen?"

Mom stood and crossed over to the sofa with the bird-of-paradise slipcover. Her old brown suitcase lay open on top of it, half-full of clothes. It was the same suitcase she'd taken when we'd snuck out of Chautauqua County at midnight last year.

"We haven't got much time," she said as she folded a pair

of pants. "I need you to go to your room, get out of those wet clothes, and pack everything you can in the bag I put on your bed. Clothes and toiletries are a priority. And make sure your sister is getting her own butt in gear too."

"Why?" I pleaded. None of this made any sense, and none of it was helping keep my heart from banging right out of my body. "Why do we have to leave now? What's going on?"

Mom stopped folding and tilted her head. "Oh, Pepper-nose, I'm so sorry. I thought you knew. The river's flooding because of all this rain. It's already crested the bank, and they think it's going to reach the trailer park by midnight."

"The river?" I mumbled, too numb to think straight.

"We've got no choice," she said, and continued packing. "The town's set up a temporary shelter in the high school gym. We'll stay there until this passes and, God willing, we can return. Now, don't just stand there. I want to be clear of here within the hour. *Git!*"

I headed to my room, but my brain was spinning wildly. Why was this happening? Things had seemed so wonderful only a few minutes before. I'd torn up all the Rules, I'd had an actual conversation with Mr. Capp, and something like one with Maddie of all people. Then a flood had to barge in and make a mess of one of the best days ever. I just couldn't catch a break.

Then again, I figured one good thing would come from the rising waters. I wouldn't have to pull Hush-a-bye out of the trash and toss her in the river because the river was coming to take her back all on its own. So maybe it wasn't such a bad day after all.

The cold damp of my clothes stuck to my skin, and I shivered. I grabbed a towel from the bathroom, then headed into our bedroom, eager to dry off. Antonia sat on the far edge of her bed with her back to me, her head bent forward.

"Mom says we need to get moving, Antonia," I said. Antonia didn't say anything.

I peeled off the wet clothes, toweled myself off, and put on dry jeans and a sweater. Antonia hadn't moved the whole time.

"Come on." I tossed the wet towel against her back. She didn't budge. I shrugged and raked a comb through my hair. "We're going to hang out in the high school gym. Doesn't that sound like fun?"

Antonia lifted her head but still didn't look at me. When she spoke, her voice sounded strange, like she was struggling to get the words out.

"What did you do to Hush-a-bye?"

I stopped combing and swallowed. Why would she ask a question like that? She must have forgotten the story I'd told her that morning, but something about the strangled tone of her voice unsettled me. Still, I figured she was probably worried about the flood and what would happen to all her precious treasures, including that awful doll.

I had planned to tell her the whole truth about Hush-a-

bye right then, but with the floodwaters coming and us need-
ing to get out, it didn't seem like the best time to come clean
and get into a big battle over what I'd done. So I stuck with
the original fib.

"I told you, she's in my drawer so Mom wouldn't find
her," I said. "Don't worry, I'll pack her away with my stuff."

Lightning lit up the sky. For a brief moment, I could see
the limbs of the ginkgo tree thrashing through our bedroom
window. And right then, Antonia let loose a scream that shot
like an electric current through my whole body. It wasn't her
usual howler-monkey squeal either. There was nothing joyful in it at all—just pure, wild rage.

Antonia leaped off her bed and spun about. Her face was
red, and her teeth were gritted. I'd never seen her look so
angry, and it scared me.

It didn't take me long to figure out why she was mad. I
saw the limp thing she was cradling in her arms like a
wounded animal.

She'd found Hush-a-bye.

24

A FEW GREASE stains spotted the doll's dress, and her hair was matted. But what really caught my attention were the two brand-new arms attached to her body. And those bright, bitter green eyes.

I've got you now, they seemed to say. *I've got you right where I want you.*

"What did you do to Hush-a-bye?" Antonia repeated.

"Antonia, please," I said, trying and failing to keep the shaking out of my voice. "I was going to tell you when I got home."

"Liar," Antonia spat out. A violent thunderclap shook the bedroom window.

"Listen to me," I begged. "She's not what you think she is. She tried to hurt someone I know at school, and I mean hurt real bad. We've got to get rid of her before she hurts someone else."

"Liar!" Antonia screamed. She hugged the doll tight to

her chest. "Hush-a-bye told me everything. Everything! You tried to make her attack your friend, and then . . . then you threw her in the trash when she wouldn't. If she hadn't called for me, I never would have found her."

"It wasn't like that at all," I said.

"So how did she get in the trash can? Did she walk there?" She sneered and glared at me like I was some stranger. Part of me wanted to slap her face. But the other part just crumbled to pieces.

"Antonia, you don't understand," I pleaded.

"You think I'm stupid, like Zoogie said." Antonia's bottom lip quivered. "I'm *not* stupid. I heard Hush-a-bye calling for me and I found her and she told me what you'd done." Tears ran down her face. "You lied to me, Lucy. Why did you lie to me? Why?"

The pained look in Antonia's face tore me up inside. But I heard the rain lash hard against the trailer roof, and a picture flashed in my mind of the Susquehanna swelling up the bank, crashing through the winterberry bushes and rolling toward our trailer.

The flood's coming, I thought. *We need to get out of here.*

"We haven't got time for this," I held out my hand. "Give me the doll, and we'll deal with it later."

"No!" Antonia screamed. "You're never going to take her from me again! Never! Never!"

It was pointless arguing with Antonia when she was like this. I knew I'd have to take the doll away by force if I could.

So I stepped toward Antonia to grab Hush-a-bye, when a movement in the corner of my eye caught my attention. I turned and gulped.

The small lamp on the nightstand between our beds was floating in the air.

"Antonia—"

The lamp hovered there a second, then flew straight at me. I barely had time to duck my head. The base of it grazed my scalp before it shattered against the opposite wall.

I stared at the deep dent in the wall where it struck. When I turned back to Antonia, she was smiling. *Smiling.*

"You can't tell us what to do anymore," she said.

Our bedroom door burst open. Mom stumbled in, breathing hard.

"What is all this ruckus?" she said, holding her hand to her stomach. "I do not have time for this."

Her eyes darted between the broken lamp, the unpacked bag, and the strange, legless doll Antonia clutched against her chest. Mom's mouth hung open like she couldn't figure out what to start yelling about first.

But I wasn't worried about the hurricane Mom was getting ready to unleash on us. In the spot where the lamp bashed the wall, hairline cracks had spread down to the floor and up to the ceiling. The cracks were branching out like spiderwebs, and they were growing wider.

"Make her stop, Antonia," I pleaded.

Antonia ignored me. She barged her way past Mom with

Hush-a-bye tucked under her arm and ran out of the bed-room. Mom stood there looking stunned, trying to piece to-gether all the weirdness swirling about in the room. But when the door slammed behind her, she whipped about with a buzz-saw fury.

"Oh, no you don't." She rattled the knob and banged on the door, but it wouldn't budge. The cracks multiplied across the ceiling.

"Open this door right now, young lady, or you are going to be in a lifetime of trouble!" Mom yelled as she pounded on the door. "Are you listening to me?"

Plaster dust sputtered out of the widening cracks. The small window in the top corner of our room broke in half and fell outside. Rain whipped through the open space and ran down the cracked wall while lightning and thunder chewed up the sky.

Mom was so caught up in getting the door open she didn't notice any of it. I grabbed her arm.

"Mom, we've got to get out," I said, and pulled at her. She turned at me and glared.

"Don't you tell me—" Then her eyes took in the whole mosaic of cracks crisscrossing the room, and the color drained from her face. "Oh, dear lord," she whispered.

The walls began to hum. The hum changed to the groan of buckling aluminum. A jagged chunk of the ceiling broke away and crashed on Antonia's bed. Mom screamed.

I knew what was coming. I'd seen how Hush-a-bye tried

to murder Maddie. Now it was my turn, and there was no one around to stop her. Even if Mom got hurt too.

I frantically scanned the room for an exit. The door was locked. The window was too small and covered in broken glass. We were trapped like moths in a killing jar. With no time left to find another way out. I had to do something.

So I leaped forward and wrapped my arms around my mom, and with a strength I never knew I had, I dragged her to the floor between the beds as the walls caved in and the ceiling collapsed and the trailer crashed down on top of us.

25

AFTER A STUNNED moment, I blinked my eyes against the swirling dust and driving rain and saw nothing but blackness. "Mom?" I shouted into the darkness. There was no response. "Mom? Mom! Can you hear me?"

I'd had her in my arms when we fell between the beds, but I'd lost my grip on her when the ceiling and walls came down like an avalanche. Now I didn't know where she was.

"Mom! Say something. *Please.*"

My shoulder was pressed up against something cold and hard. I figured it must be one of the bed railings. I moved my hands around me. Pieces of what felt like waterlogged drywall and aluminum siding covered my legs. I yanked them off as best I could and pulled my feet up.

I shifted to my hands and knees and slowly crawled forward, brushing debris out of the way. Every so often a sharp something would stab me and I'd pull back in pain. But I kept going.

"Mom, where are you?" I pleaded.

When I got to the end of the other bed, I felt something soft and damp in my fingers. With a shiver, I realized it was hair.

I scrambled forward, heaving chunks of the trailer out of the way, and ran my hands over my mother's face.

"Wake up, Mom," I said, patting her cheeks frantically. "Please wake up."

She didn't move. I couldn't feel any breath coming out of her nose or mouth. She was so cold, so lifeless. I moved my hands down to her chest. I couldn't locate a heartbeat.

Every nerve in my body wanted to scream *You can't die, you can't die!* I pressed my fingers to the side of her neck. It was slow and faint, but there was a pulse. A sob bubbled out of me, and I leaned down and kissed her on the cheek.

"Help! Antonia!" I yelled into the darkness and the storm. "Please, somebody, help!"

I screamed myself hoarse while the rain beat the ground and my mom lay unmoving under my hands. My throat was raw, and I felt numb and cold down to my bones. My head slumped forward, and all I wanted to do was lie down next to my mother and close my eyes.

Then several dim flickers of light appeared in the distance, like large fireflies. They grew closer, and I could make out the hazy beams of flashlights.

"Here!" I managed to get out in a hoarse whisper. "Over here!"

Several shouting voices filled the air. Sounds of sloshing

and debris crunching underfoot joined them. A pair of unseen hands lifted me up. I reached out to Mom and cried.

"Don't worry," a man's voice said in my ear. "They'll take good care of her. Let's get you to the EMT."

I was led to the back of an ambulance and told to sit on a large metal box. The bright interior lights stung my eyes.

A woman in green rain gear and yellow boots examined me. She wrapped a thin foil blanket around my shoulders. It was surprisingly warm, but I couldn't stop shivering.

"Is that your mom?" she asked. I nodded. "She's going to be okay. Looks like part of a wall or something hit her in the head and knocked her out. She'll be fine, but we'll need to take her to the hospital."

She held a pen flashlight to my eyes and looked at each one in turn. "Doesn't look like you received any head injury. Just a few scratches and bruises. I've got to say, you're both pretty lucky. We've been riding about the neighborhood, helping those too sick to evacuate on their own, when one of our crew spotted the wreckage." She gestured over her shoulder. "What happened out there? Some kind of sinkhole, I'd guess, though I didn't think the floodwaters had come far enough for something like that."

"I—I don't know," I said.

"Is it just you and your mom?"

My heart skipped a beat. "No. My sister. She ran outside before our house . . ." I swallowed and fought back new tears. "I don't know where she is."

A grim look passed over the woman's face, and then she quickly replaced it with a smile.

"How old is she?"

"Eleven. She has a sparkly baby-duck barrette in her hair."

She laid her hand on my cheek. "Don't you worry. We'll find her. You wait here and rest. I'll be back in a few minutes." She jumped down from the ambulance and shut the doors behind her.

All was still except for the constant thump of the rain against the roof. I pulled the foil blanket tight around my body. Every inch of me was either cold or hurt or both. Mostly both.

"Why did she have to find that doll?" I muttered to myself. And then I remembered something Antonia had said—*If she hadn't called for me, I never would have found her.*

Hush-a-bye *called* to her. That meant she must have spoken to Antonia somehow from inside the trash can, like they had some kind of mental connection. But if that was the case, why didn't she say anything to Antonia the night I took her from the closet? Or for that matter, why didn't she talk to Antonia all that time after that mess with the Gypsum Man? Unless—

"Unless that's exactly how she planned it," I whispered.

The truth hit me like a two-ton truck. That weird dream that scared me so much about what Hush-a-bye might do next, and how she never fought back when I'd stolen her from the closet and hid her in the trash can—it was all a setup. That scheming doll *meant* for me to throw her out. She'd set the whole thing in motion after I'd threatened to tear her head off for hurting Maddie. She knew how to turn my own sister against me, and make me look like the bad guy.

But all that didn't answer an even bigger question knocking about my skull—did Antonia know what Hush-a-bye had just done to me and Mom?

I knew when Antonia got mad, her brain overheated and what good sense she had boiled away. But destroying the trailer with us still inside? We might have been killed. No matter how angry she might be, she wouldn't ever wish that on us. Would she?

"It doesn't matter," I said, deciding to set the question aside for the moment. "I've got to get her away from that doll."

I threw off the foil blanket. Helpful as those ambulance people were, I knew they'd never find Antonia. She didn't want to be found, and besides, Hush-a-bye wouldn't let it happen.

Then again, how was I going to find them? I didn't have the faintest idea where they'd gone. I grunted and kicked my heel against the metal box.

A puddle of water pooled at my dripping feet, and I dragged my toe across the puddle. It made a small stream that disappeared into a drain on the vehicle floor. I stared as it flowed down.

"Like a river," I said.

A flood of memories washed over me all at once. The first day I stumbled across the doll's head. The rowboat that took us to find Hush-a-bye's body. The old photo of Rosetta clutching the familiar doll before going missing. They all led back to the same place.

"The island." I banged my fist against the box. "They're going to Hunter's Moon Island."

I considered tracking down one of the adults to tell them and get a search party going, but quickly scratched the idea. I was sure no one would believe me. The story was too ridiculous. They'd think I was hallucinating after bumping my head, and they'd ship me off to the hospital for X-rays. I'd never get to the island then.

Besides, by time I found someone, told them about the island, and a search party was organized, it might be too late for Antonia. Too late for what, I wasn't sure—or didn't want to think about. No, I had to go myself.

Now.

I managed to dig up a flashlight from an emergency pack, along with a heavy-duty rain poncho. But it was what I found under the poncho that really got my attention: safety matches and a bottle of rubbing alcohol.

The thunderstorm, I thought. There was a detail in Rosetta's story I hadn't thought about too much at the time, but seeing the matches and alcohol brought it back. When the hotel caught fire, Hush-a-bye had wanted to get away from there as quick as possible. Why? *Because she was afraid of fire.*

That must be it. That must be her weakness. Everyone has one. Even Superman can be knocked out if you slip some Kryptonite in his cornflakes.

The label on the rubbing alcohol warned it was flammable and to avoid contact with an open flame. I hoped the label wasn't lying. I remembered the red sash was still in my pocket. I pulled it out and set it on the floor of the ambulance. I poured some of the rubbing alcohol on it, struck one of the safety matches, and dropped it. The sash instantly burst into flames.

"That'll do nicely," I said, wrinkling my nose at the pungent smoke rising up as I stomped out the shriveled, blackened sash.

I scrapped my plan to throw Hush-a-bye back into the river. She was too dangerous to let some other unsuspecting girl find her and start the whole mess all over again. This had to end tonight, forever. I'd have to burn her down until she was nothing but ashes.

26

I CAREFULLY OPENED the back of the ambulance and peeked outside. Feet stamped back and forth and voices called out through the rain, but no one was close enough to notice me. I slipped out, shut the door, and crept down toward the winterberry bushes behind the rubble of our trailer.

By the time I reached the path, the river was already up to my ankles. I sloshed though the frigid water and pointed the flashlight into the nest of dense undergrowth. Somewhere inside that mess was the little rowboat Antonia and I had hidden after we returned from the island. I planned to use it to get across. Unfortunately, with the rain pouring down like a waterfall, I could barely see a foot in front of me.

Then another thought stopped me short. What if Antonia had already taken the boat? Or what if it had been caught up in the floodwaters and drifted away? How would I get across to the island without a boat?

"I'll swim if I have to," I muttered to myself, but I didn't feel as brave as I tried to sound. And after another ten minutes of searching through wet plants, all I came up with were wrinkled fingers. Finally giving up on the boat, I trudged down the path toward the riverbank.

I was already chilled to the bone from the endless rain and the floodwater sloshing against my thighs. Plunging into the Susquehanna was bound to be even colder. But I still plodded forward to the bank, or at least the place I guessed the bank used to be. I didn't have a clue what I'd do once I reached it, but I hoped I'd think of something once I got there.

The water was soon past my hips. It was like walking through icy slush, and my feet felt like they weighed ten pounds each. With each step, the mud grabbed hold tight and didn't want to let go.

I tried to remember how far it was to Hunter's Moon Island. One hundred feet? Two hundred? Half a mile? The more I thought about it the farther away it seemed.

My right foot caught in a thick patch of mud. I tried to pull it out, but it wouldn't budge. I tucked the plastic bag and flashlight under one arm and tried to lift my leg out with both hands.

"Come on, come on." My hands strained in the icy water, my fingers numb as stones. Then my foot suddenly popped out, and I fell backward. My arms flailed wildly, and the flashlight and bag tumbled away.

"Ouch!"

My bottom struck something hard. I rubbed my aching rear end, but the pain there was pretty quickly forgotten once I realized something about this situation didn't make sense. I reached out to touch the ground around me. It felt rocky and completely dry.

How could that be? And why wasn't I splashing about and choking on dirty river water? Where did the river go?

I spotted the flashlight and the plastic bag on the ground nearby and scrambled over to them. I snatched up the bag, flicked on the flashlight, and circled the beam around my feet.

The water was gone. There wasn't even a puddle. I wondered if I'd stumbled upon some kind of ledge or sandbar. But then I trained the light off to the side and sucked in my breath. I found the river.

Like Moses parting the Red Sea, the river was pushed back on both sides, held in place by some kind of invisible wall. A five-foot space separated the two halves of the river, and the rocky path of the riverbed was exposed in between.

I could only make out about twenty feet ahead of me, but I knew the path would go all the way up to the island. This was Hush-a-bye's work, no doubt. But it didn't make sense. Why would she make it easier for me to get to her and Antonia?

I came up with two possibilities. One was she'd let me get halfway across before letting the river drop back down and drown me. It was not a comforting thought.

There was a second possibility, though. It wasn't much better than the first, but somehow it made the most sense. Hush-a-bye made the path because she knew I'd come after Antonia and she was waiting for me on the island. Judging from the humiliating ways she'd punished the lunch lady, Gus, Zoogie, and Maddie, drowning me quietly didn't seem like her style. Whatever pain she had planned for me, I'm sure she'd want to have a front-row seat to watch it happen.

This was a bad, bad situation. The smart thing would have been to run away as fast as my legs would carry me and let the adults handle this. But the smart thing wasn't an option for me. Antonia was my little baby sister, no matter what she'd done. I had to find her *now*, before something terrible happened to her. And so I started running up the path across the riverbed.

I had a lot on my mind then, so it took a minute before I realized the rain wasn't drenching me anymore. I looked up. The rain was still beating down just as viciously as it had been, but some unseen barrier held it back several feet above my head. If I wasn't so scared, I might have been grateful. Except I knew Hush-a-bye didn't do anything out of kindness. Maybe it was to remind me she could do anything she wanted—even control the rain.

The ground dipped as I made my way toward the middle of the river. Pieces of garbage dumped in the water over the years were scattered among the rocks—gas cans, car tires, even a raggedy baby stroller.

The flashlight beam caught something big thrashing on the river floor a few feet ahead. It was long and black and snakelike, except the head looked like it had been squashed. I crept up closer, holding my breath.

I let it out once I saw it was only a mud-devil salamander, somehow left behind when the river slipped to the side. I'd only ever glimpsed the tail of one, and I'd never seen a whole one up close. It was dark green with light brown spots, and it had glassy eyes and a wide mouth that gulped for the vanished water.

I set the flashlight on the ground and scooped my hands under the mud devil. It was even uglier up close, but I knew it was harmless. Its breathing was shallow, and it didn't squirm too much. I wondered if I was too late to save it.

I carried it to the wall of water and pressed its head against it. For a moment, it just lay there with its head in the river and its body in my hands. But then, with a quick snap, the creature shot through the wall and disappeared into the black water.

I set my palm against the water wall. The current trembled across my skin. For a tiny moment, I thought about pushing my face through the wall. After all, when would I ever get another chance to see the river like that?

But then I pictured myself sucked in by the current and the river carrying me away, then Mom waking up in a hospital, frantically banging on the nurse's button while calling out for her firecrackers. And Antonia—

I shook the thought out of my head, and I started running.

The ground began to slope upward. I could just make out the low scrub and grassy bank of the Hunter's Moon Island shore but not the birch trees.

I jogged farther up the island bank and took a breath. Then water splashed against the back of my leg and I turned about. The path I'd just traveled through was gone. The churning river water of the Susquehanna had fallen back in place.

"Well, at least I didn't get caught in the water," I said to myself, but it was cold comfort. I trudged up to the top of slope, not sure what would happen next, not sure who or what I'd find there waiting for me. I thought I was ready for anything. But when I finally reached the top of the slope, what I saw there stopped me dead in my tracks.

"Oh my," I said.

The flashlight dropped out of my hand and rolled back down the slope into the river. It was sucked into the current and disappeared.

It didn't matter. I wouldn't need it to find my way around the island any more than I'd need it to find Antonia. I could see where she'd gone, clear as the noonday sun.

With legs like cement, I plodded slowly up the grassy bank. Buttery yellow light spilled across the freshly mowed lawn. The bright glow came from the long, two-storied bank of windows, every single one lit up like the Fourth of July.

Hunter's Moon Lodge had come back to the island.

27

I'D SEEN A lot of weird things since finding the doll's head, but this was a whole other level of strangeness, like finding Narnia in the back of the wardrobe or stepping out of a tornado into Munchkinland.

Part of me wondered if I was still trapped under the collapsed trailer, sunk in a deep coma and dream-walking the river while my face was half-buried in the mud. But this was no dream.

It was all there. The long white two-story building dotted with brightly lit windows and sturdy columns. The same jumble of tinny piano music, grown-up voices, and laughter drifting across the grounds.

Off to one side of the lodge was the forked tree where we'd found Hush-a-bye's body. It looked as dead as ever, its branches still curled over like witch's fingers. The red rowboat that took Antonia and me over to Hush-a-bye's body was sitting at its base. I walked over and peeked inside the boat.

On the center bench was a small leather suitcase. With trembling fingers, I undid the latch and opened it. Inside was a block of green foam with two long indents cut out of it. Whatever was in the spaces had been taken out, but it seemed to me two doll legs would have fit in them perfectly. I gripped the plastic bag tighter.

I stepped carefully onto the long porch. It creaked. I placed my palm on one of the columns. The wood felt cool and smooth and very solid.

I approached a large, dark-stained door with frosted windows and a long brass handle. The music sounded louder now, and the voices too, but I couldn't clearly make out what was being said.

I breathed in slowly and let it out like it was the last breath I'd ever take. Then I opened the door.

The voices and music stopped abruptly, like someone had pressed the mute button. I stepped in the lobby of the hotel, but no one was there. I closed the door and leaned back against it, then reminded myself to start breathing again.

Just like my dream, the hotel had a front lobby desk with a bell on top, a winding staircase with a polished banister, and a chandelier above it all, shining like a thousand brilliant diamonds. The musty, sharp smell, like a mix of damp earth and moldy leaves, was something new. But I never smelled anything in my dream.

"Antonia?" I called out in a small voice. No response. I stepped away from the door and stood in the silence, waiting for something. What that something was, I wasn't sure. I wasn't sure I wanted to find out either.

"Antonia," I called out again, a little louder. Still no answer. I opened the plastic bag to make sure the bottle of rubbing alcohol and safety matches were still there.

I knew they would be. I was stalling. Because I was terrified. Whatever haunted this place was surely waiting for me up the staircase and down the long hallway. Just like in my dream. I swallowed, tucked the bag under my arm, and headed up the stairs. For Antonia.

I held on to the banister as tightly as I could while I climbed. It wasn't easy. It felt smooth as glass, and my hand kept slipping. Not that I really needed its support. The stairs weren't too steep, and I wasn't in any danger of falling if I let go. But it felt good to have something solid to hold on to.

Each step groaned as my foot pressed down on it. The sound echoed throughout the empty lobby. I glanced quickly over my shoulder, imagining someone was following me, but no one was there.

"Get a grip, get a grip," I whispered to myself, squeezing my nails painfully into my palm.

At the top of staircase where the second-floor hallway began, a rectangle of white light glowed. I kept my eyes glued on it with each step.

"Almost there," I said. It wasn't the most comforting thought.

A small shadow moved into the light. I stopped. Then a

voice that might have been Antonia's—or something trying
to sound like Antonia—started singing.

> *Hush-a-bye and good night*
> *Till the bright morning light*
> *Takes the sleep from your eyes*
> *Hush-a-bye, baby bright*

"Antonia?" I called out. The shadow drew back into the
hallway.

"Antonia! Wait!" I sprinted up the rest of stairs, my heart
banging against my chest.

When I reached the top, I turned to the right. The same
hallway I'd dreamed about stretched out impossibly long
ahead of me. I pinched my earlobe to make sure I was still
awake. It hurt, so yep, not a dream. The sound of a door shut-
ting echoed from the far end of it.

"You can do this, you can do this," I muttered to myself
as I pinched my lobe painfully one more time, just to make
sure.

My feet made swishing sounds against the carpet as I ran
down the hall. I avoided looking at the doors I passed, ashy
white with stark black numbers at the top. It felt like they
were staring at me as I approached each one, sizing me up. I
listened for whispers but heard nothing.

After what seemed like forever, I finally reached the end
of the hallway. And there, just like I knew they would be,

were the double French doors from my dream. I was here at last. Whoever, or whatever, was waiting for me was behind them.

I couldn't stop shaking. I was more scared than I'd ever been. But it didn't matter. I was here to rescue Antonia, even if I had only the faintest idea anymore how to do it. I turned the handle and opened the doors.

The room was dark and cold. The only light was dim and gray and came through a bay window in the back. I could hear the muffled sound of rain beating against the pane. A silhouette blocked the light in the center of the window.

"Antonia?" I whispered. There was no response, but I caught a glint from what looked like her sparkly duckling barrette. My heart raced.

I've found her, I thought. *Thank God for that ugly barrette. I'd know it anywhere.*

"It's me, Antonia. It's Lucy." The silhouette didn't make a sound.

I stepped inside. The doors clicked shut behind me. I turned my head and considered trying the handles to see if they'd still open, but there didn't seem to be any point. Either I was trapped or I wasn't, and there wasn't much I could do about it right then.

I took another step forward, and the lights clicked on. I blinked and raised my hand to my eyes. A large, globe-shaped chandelier illuminated an empty room with faded blue walls and a parquet floor.

Antonia sat cross-legged on a cushioned ledge under the bay window. The doll sat in her lap. Her long, curly hair was brushed in front of her face. Two bright pink legs with shiny black shoes jutted out from the bottom of her dress—Hush-a-bye's reward for dropping the trailer on Mom and me, I guessed.

Antonia held a hairbrush in her hand. She was focused on the slow, even brushing motion she made through the doll's hair. I swallowed hard. "Antonia, are you all right?"

She said nothing but kept on brushing. Her eyes were glazed and unfocused, like she was half-asleep.

A streak of lightning shot through the sky like it was splitting it in half, followed by loud crack of thunder. Antonia didn't even flinch. "I've come here to get you," I said. "I want you to come home with me."

Antonia stopped brushing. Her fingers trembled slightly. I reached out my hand to my sister, ready to take hold of hers.

The doll's head snapped up. Her hair fell to the sides, and two bottomless, bright green eyes stared back at me.

"We *are* home," Hush-a-bye said.

28

HUSH-A-BYE'S VOICE WAS thick, like someone trying to talk through a mouthful of mud—the same voice I'd heard through the closet door and in my dream.

I tried to sound calmer than I felt. "Please, Antonia," I said, tearing my eyes away from the doll and back to my sister. "We've got to go. The river's rising."

Antonia didn't answer. She wouldn't even look in my direction. Thunder rumbled far away, and rain thudded against the roof.

I tried to step forward, but damp, heavy hands pushed down hard on my shoulders. I fell to my knees and let out a yelp. When I looked over my shoulder to see who was holding me down, no one was there. But I knew it was Hush-a-bye's doing.

"You've got your legs," I said, looking right at Hush-a-bye. "You're all put together now. Why don't you let Antonia go? What do you need her for?"

Hush-a-bye grinned. Her teeth were small and pointed and covered with wet green moss. Her face wasn't a doll's face anymore. But it wasn't human either.

A sickly sweet smell came off her, like dead tulips decaying in a vase. A fierce clap of thunder, closer than before, rattled the window. Antonia still hadn't budged, but a long ribbon of goose bumps popped up along her bare arms.

Something I couldn't see yanked away the plastic bag with the rubbing alcohol and the box of safety matches. It skittered across the floor and came to a rest at Antonia's feet.

"Look what she brings us," Hush-a-bye said. "Fire and destruction. Just as I told you."

"That's not true!" I cried out. "Hush-a-bye's the one who's a monster. She's the one who destroyed our trailer. She nearly killed Mom and me. Mom is in the hospital!"

"Lies, lies," Hush-a-bye said, shaking her head. "Everything she's ever told us is lies."

"Antonia, you know I'd never hurt you," I said. She didn't answer. "Antonia?" My voice cracked. "You know I wouldn't, don't you?"

Her head slumped forward, and she pressed her hands against her seat. The hairbrush clattered to the floor.

I bolted forward. Nothing held me back this time. The invisible hands pressing down on me before were gone. I scrambled on my hands and knees toward the bay window, grabbed Hush-a-bye by the neck, and flung her away as hard as I could. There was a loud crack against the wall, but I didn't bother to look over. Instead, I took hold of Antonia's wrists.

"Listen, Antonia," I pleaded, trying and failing to catch my sister's eyes. "I came here to save you. I promise I would never do anything to hurt you. Ever. I love you. Please come with me."

Antonia sat there like a clod of dirt, not responding in any way. A huge aching wave filled my chest.

"Please, Antonia," I said, tears running down my face. "I know I lied to you. It rips me up how much I hurt you. So here's the truth, all of it. I don't have friends. I don't talk to anyone. No one talks to me. Every day at school I'm scared and lonely and sad, and it hurts so bad I can hardly get through one day to the next." I sobbed and pressed my cheek against her leg. "All I've got is you and Mom. I need you, Antonia. I need you so bad."

I started to reach out for Antonia's face, when the clammy, invisible hands jerked me back, sliding me across the floor to where I'd been a moment ago. Antonia's chin was still pressed against her chest, eyes hidden, her hands now curled between her knees.

"Poor, poor Lucy." I turned to the familiar mud-filled voice. Hush-a-bye was sitting with her back against the wall, her mossy teeth grinning like a moldy jack-o'-lantern. "All she wants is love, even if it means breaking my head open to get it. *But I don't break that easily.*"

I stared at Hush-a-bye. Now I understood why the

invisible hands had let me go. She knew I'd try to get her away from Antonia. She wanted Antonia to see it. To turn her against me even more.

I felt as hollowed out as a rotten log. My sister wouldn't look at me or speak to me. She didn't believe me. She wanted nothing more to do with me. I'd lost her.

Hush-a-bye leered at me, her green eyes glowing. "You see, Antonia? She's got nothing but brutality and lies," she said. "We're done listening. It is time to go."

The French doors flew open behind me. And there in the hallway, where there had only been a bare wall when I entered, was the huge iron door from my dream. It was covered with the same fish bones and thick vines I remembered. But this time four rusted bolts were set along the right side of the door.

The top one slid open with a grating sound—*skreeee*. Dark water leaked from beneath the door. I could almost feel its iciness filling my lungs.

Just outside the window, a streak of lightning shot down and struck a tall birch, lopping off a branch. The lights in the room flickered and went out.

Another bolt scraped open. *Skreeee*. In the darkness, Hush-a-bye's mud-filled voice oozed into my head.

"Antonia's with me now. Forever and ever. Like my dear Rosetta would have been . . . until she betrayed me." Hush-a-bye let out a low growl like a dog getting ready to pounce. "She was weak and stupid. No better than the rest of the filth who pollute this world. No better than you, who wanted to throw me away the first moment we met."

Skreeee.

"But Antonia . . ." Hush-a-bye sighed. "I knew she was the one I had been waiting for. She called out to me right away, called out to have me punish the wicked ones. And each time she called for me, I grew stronger. Soon, this very night, I'll be strong enough to lay waste to every last miserable soul who dares defy us. Then it will be just the two of us. Forever and ever."

Skreeee. The last bolt. I closed my eyes and shivered.

"But first, on this special night," Hush-a-bye said, her voice no more than a whisper, "I'll show you what the midnight stars look like from the bottom of the river. Good night, Lucy, sleep tight."

The hands began dragging me out through the French doors. I could feel the frigid water on my legs and hear the thrashing of river against the iron door and the groan of its hinges as it started to open. I didn't resist. What for? There wasn't anything left to do. Hush-a-bye had won.

Then a small voice whispered faintly, far back in the dark room. "I'm so sorry, Lucy." The lights flickered on. And the sight that greeted me nearly took my last breath away.

No longer sitting on the bay window seat, Antonia was crouched on the floor with knees bent, the plastic bag crumpled at her feet. The box of safety matches was tucked under one arm, and in her hands she gripped the bottle of rubbing alcohol and pointed it straight at Hush-a-bye. And then Antonia squeezed it.

A gush of clear liquid shot out. Hush-a-bye tried to slide away from it, but her body didn't cooperate. She stumbled onto her side, howling and sputtering. The alcohol hit her square in the face, dousing her and the surrounding floor. Its sharp odor pinched my nose.

Antonia dropped the empty bottle and took hold of the safety matches, her lips pressed tightly together. She drew one out and sparked it into a steady flame.

"Whatever she's done, she's my sister, and I'm not going to let you throw her in the river like trash," Antonia said. "You let her leave or you'll go up like fireworks."

Hush-a-bye tried to push herself off the floor, a strangled gurgling coming from her throat. The blond curls, matted and dripping, slid off her head like a wig as she struggled to sit up. They fell with a thick plop on the floor. Scabby red patches covered her skull.

"Deceit, deceit," she hissed.

The doll lifted her head and glared at Antonia. I shuddered. The green was all gone from her eyes. Everything was gone from them. They weren't even black—just two liquid pools of emptiness.

"Nothing but lies and deceit surround me." Her hateful, hollow eyes grew large as half-dollars. "You think I'm some toy you can toss aside when you're tired of playing?" She grinned, and green spittle dribbled down her chin. "Let me show you my real face."

A jagged crack split Hush-a-bye's face from the top of her head down to her chin. Oily brown liquid oozed out. She jammed her fingers into the crack and pulled it apart. With a sound like breaking bones, the doll's head ripped clean in two.

"Throw the match!" I cried. But Antonia just stood there with deer-in-the-headlights glazed eyes.

A monstrous mushroom-shaped head unfolded from the stump of the neck like some nightmarish balloon. It rose all the way up to the ceiling, then bent down and split from side to side, revealing a gaping mouth with dozens of jagged, spear-point teeth.

"Throw it, Antonia!" I shouted. "Now!"

But all the courage and confidence had drained from Antonia's face. The lit match was burning down close to her fingertips. I tried to run to her, but I couldn't move. The invisible hands still held me tight.

"Throw it!" I screamed in desperation. "Antonia, throw the match!"

Hush-a-bye's doll body burst apart. The dress scattered about in shreds, and tendrils like steel cables spiked with hooked thorns wriggled out and wormed their way across the floor.

One of them reached Antonia and wrapped itself around

her ankle. She looked at in in a daze, like she couldn't believe it was really happening.

I strained against the invisible hands' grip. "Don't look at it! Look at me!"

Another tendril grabbed her other ankle. The hooked thorns dug into her skin, but she didn't seem to notice the pain. She just looked lost. The head let loose a howl that rattled the windows. The tendrils began pulling Antonia in, closer to the gaping mouth and rows of churning teeth. The match was nearly out. I had to do something.

"*Antonia Willa Bloom!*" I yelled in a fierce voice that would have done our mother proud. "You'd better throw that match right now or I'm going to tell Mom, and then you'll be in *so much trouble!*"

Antonia blinked and turned to me with a bewildered look. For a single half second that felt like a hundred years, she just stared at me. But then I saw Antonia's brain finally click into gear.

She bit her bottom lip and closed her eyes. With a flick of her wrist, she tossed the smoldering match. We all watched as it arced through the air and landed on one of the tendrils. It hissed, a thin line of smoke rose . . . and the match went out.

29

MUFFLED LAUGHTER RUMBLED from the wicked mouth as it rocked back and forth high above us. Antonia stared intently at the wisp of smoke as it curled up, and she pinched at her bottom lip. She turned to me and whispered, "What do we do now?"

I smiled weakly and whispered, "It's okay, Antonia," even as the invisible hands, tight around my arms, began to drag me out once more, icy water sloshing on my legs. "I found you and you came back to me. That's all that matters."

We'd almost done it. We'd almost won. I'd come here to get back Antonia, and in a way, I guess I had. She'd tried to save me like I'd tried to save her. If nothing else, Hush-a-bye failed to change her into a monster like she was.

We were sisters and we had each other's backs, and no demon from hell could take that away from us. It was something, anyway. I think Antonia must have thought so too, because she paid back my smile with a wide grin of her own.

Except that grin was a little too big.

I was on the threshold of the French doors with the cold water practically up to my hips, wondering how long I could hold my breath until the river swallowed me up forever, and Antonia was grinning. *Grinning.* For a horrible two seconds that lasted about ten years, I thought she'd gone back under Hush-a-bye's sway.

Then I saw why she was grinning.

A small blue flame no bigger than a nickel had sputtered and poked up from the floor like a baby cobra climbing out of its shell. And it was growing, larger and larger and brighter and brighter.

Abruptly, the monster stopped laughing. The tendrils frantically unwrapped themselves from Antonia's legs. They beat down again and again at the lick of flame, but every time the lick was walloped, two more sprang up and joined together to make an even larger one. The fire was spreading fast.

The water around my legs suddenly drained away, and the invisible hands holding me let go. I fell forward onto a floor that was a shade hotter than a vinyl car seat in July. I shrieked and scrambled to my feet, quickly glancing out to the hallway as I patted my legs. The iron door had disappeared. I rushed over to Antonia, who was watching the show in front of her with a wild-eyed stare.

The monster was now covered in yellow-orange flames. It thrashed wildly from side to side, shrieking like a banshee.

Its tendrils lashed out, smashing against the ceiling and walls, and charred plaster rained everywhere. The stench of burning rot filled my nose, while smoke and super-hot air scorched my lungs.

"We've got to get out," I croaked, coughing, and took hold of Antonia's hand. Antonia nodded once, still staring, and let me drag her out.

We stumbled out of the French doors and made our way down the hallway, both of us coughing violently. The air grew cooler the farther away we got from the room, and the smoke faded.

"I think we're okay," I said. Once again, I was wrong.

Sounds of shattering glass and splintering wood erupted behind us. We jerked our heads around.

"Doesn't look okay," Antonia said.

At the end of the hallway, a huge red mass of raging fire had smashed through the French doors. It crawled toward us like a crazed lump of magma on flaming tentacles. Wallpaper curled and shriveled up, and doors exploded off their hinges as it passed. And through the mad red blob of flame, I could still see the rows and rows of dagger teeth grinding and gnashing.

Antonia and I exchanged the same *what the crap!* look. And we started running.

By the time we made it to the top of the staircase, my lungs felt like all the air had been squeezed out of them. Beside me, Antonia was panting. The fire creature was a hundred feet away, but I could feel its searing heat on the back of my neck. I glanced down the staircase. It looked so much longer than I remembered!

"Be quick, but be careful," I warned as we raced down. Antonia's fingers tightened around mine. About halfway down, I heard a crackling sound from behind us. Red light flooded the staircase and the lobby below.

"Hurry!" I shouted.

The two of us, no longer thinking about being cautious, scrambled to get away. We threw ourselves into a wild dash down the steps. Near the bottom, I lost my balance and pitched forward onto the lobby floor, dragging Antonia with me.

The staircase groaned. I looked back. The fire creature was hurling itself toward us. Banisters snapped and flew apart as it rumbled past. The carpet sizzled and smoked. The staircase heaved and bowed under the weight and the flames. Then the staircase groaned one last time, and the whole thing collapsed with the fire monster howling all the way down into the basement.

A column of dust and red flame shot up and broke against the ceiling. The floor trembled under our feet, and for a terrifying moment, I thought the whole hotel was going to fall apart.

Then a sound like hundreds of wind chimes rang out. I

looked up. The chandelier near the top of the stairs was vibrating. Each dangling crystal on it clattered against its neighbor.

The ceiling above it cracked. The shaking grew more frantic. The crack split open, and white electric sparks shot out. Then the chandelier came undone. It fell gracefully down, down, down, and crashed like a thousand water glasses being thrown to the floor at exactly the same time.

A rain of glass, embers, and burning shards poured down on me and Antonia as we crawled on our hands and knees toward what I hoped was the front entrance.

"Where's the door?" Antonia shouted. I looked around frantically. Orange light danced crazily in the lobby windows. The heat bit my skin, and thick smoke burned my nose.

"There it is!" I shouted, pointing ahead of me. We flew forward, and I yanked on the handle and the door swung open.

I pushed Antonia through and glanced back one more time. The lobby desk had collapsed. The staircase was nothing more than a jumble of broken, shattered, burning sticks surrounding a huge hole. The shards of the chandelier glowed yellow and red, and behind it the rest of the lobby was covered in flames.

And in the middle of that bonfire I could see tendrils flailing about blindly, tossing huge beams about like they were toothpicks. But for all the destruction it caused, it couldn't break free of the burning debris.

The thing howled and bellowed and roared like nothing I'd ever heard, or ever cared to hear again. It was a roiling cauldron of pain and anger, but something about how alone it was, and the uselessness of all its thrashing about, made me feel a little sorry for it. But there was nothing anyone could do for it now, so I closed the door.

Antonia stood in the darkness, looking puzzled. I ran to her.

"We've got to get out of here in case that thing gets out of the lobby," I said, grabbing her arm.

Antonia cocked her head to one side but didn't move. "I don't think that's going to happen." She pointed over my shoulder. I turned, wondering what new horrible thing was coming for us now. As it turned out, nothing was.

The hotel had vanished.

And with it, the fire, the destruction . . . and Hush-a-bye.

The tall birch trees swayed above our heads like they'd never left the island. The unscorched grass was brown and wet. A little ways off, the small red rowboat rested against the crook of the dead forked tree. Not a single sign anywhere of any hotel, let alone a burning one.

The rain had stopped. A half-moon peeked out from behind a long, thin cloud. Stars flickered in the spaces between other clouds drifting across the night sky. A hushed wind rattled the birch branches, and crickets sang in the distant scrub.

"Did we just dream all that?" Antonia asked hollowly.

I was beginning to wonder myself. But then I spotted a shallow crater in the ground where the hotel had stood. Curls of dark smoke rose lazily from it.

"What is it?" Antonia asked.

"I think I know," I said. "Come on. I don't think there's anything to worry about anymore." Even though I said it, I still felt a few prickles of doubt shiver up my spine as we approached the smoking hole.

The hole was about two feet wide, and the grass inside was black and shriveled. A charred doll's head lay in the center. Its hair had burned away, its face and shattered eyes little more than a smoldering cinder. The body, arms, and legs were nowhere to be seen.

"Oh, Hush-a-bye." Antonia choked back a sob. "Lucy, we killed Hush-a-bye."

"Don't be silly," I said in a ragged voice. "It's only a . . . an old doll's head. You can't kill a doll."

Antonia leaned over and rested her head against me.

"Lucy?" she said in a voice as quiet as I ever heard her use.

"Yeah?"

"Is Mom—"

"She'll be fine," I said. "They're taking good care of her."

"I . . . I didn't mean to hurt anyone." I could feel her whole body shaking next to me.

"I know that," I said, wrapping an arm around her waist. "Don't fret about it."

"Okay." She was quiet again, but I knew she wasn't done. "Lucy?"

"Yeah?"

"What happens now?"

Every muscle in my body hummed with pain, but I ignored it. I watched the stars and the clouds that drifted past, and the red lights of a radio transmitter on a far distant hill. I was shivering from the damp night air, but there was a warm spot deep inside me, growing bigger and bigger.

"I don't know," I said, squeezing her tight. "Whatever it is, we'll get through it together. You, me, and Mom. All for one and one for all. Like the three musketeers."

"Okay," Antonia said, "but I like Milky Ways better."

I let go of Antonia and stared at her. She looked up at me, sheepishly at first, then let her whole face bust open into a foolish grin. Soon enough we were both giggling loudly like fools, and the echo of it bounced from one hillside to the next until it sounded as if the river itself was laughing like it hadn't laughed for a long, long time.

30

IT TOOK US nearly an hour and a half for Antonia and I to get off the island. With the river running fast, it was so hard to row to the other side.

It didn't take long for the EMT folks to find us, wet and exhausted, and they took us straight to see Mom. She was a little loopy from her head injury, but we still hugged and cried. Mom stayed in the hospital a couple more days, then the county moved us into a motel until we could find another home.

The police and the medics tried to find out what happened. Antonia told a completely different story to each person she talked to. None of them fit together. Eventually, everyone gave up trying to figure out why she'd gone off on her own.

As for me, all I said was I went looking for my sister, and I found her. Which was true enough.

Mom never asked us what happened to the two of us that

night. Truth be told, the hit in the head she received did something to her memory. The whole day was a total blank to her, which really freaked her out. She didn't want to think about it too much.

The first few days in the motel were the best. We huddled under the blankets in the huge king-sized bed and clicked like mad through the three million channels on the flat-screen TV.

"Can we stay here forever?" Antonia asked.

Mom kissed her on top of her head. "Nothing I'd like better to do than to lay about with my firecrackers. But to-morrow I've got to get back to work. And you two need to get your keisters back in school."

Later that night, while Antonia was warbling in the shower, Mom sat next to me on the bed and put her arm around my shoulder. "Everything okay with you, Pepper-nose?"

"Sure," I said.

She pulled my head onto her shoulder. "I know school's been rough for you. It's not easy being picked on."

I lifted my head and stared at her. "You know about that?"

"Oh, I had a feeling," she said, and smiled sadly. "I know what it's like to be the new girl with the discount sneakers. But I figured I shouldn't interfere and you'd eventually work things out for yourself. Maybe that was wrong." She paused and rubbed my arm. "I've been thinking it would do you good to talk to somebody, you know, somebody who can listen and help you deal with all of this trouble. A nurse at the hospital was telling about a counseling program they have we might qualify for, so you could talk to someone about things at school, and friends, and . . . you know . . ."

"Living with Daddy?" I could feel her grip tighten when I said the word. "Okay, but only if you come with me."

She took a much longer pause this time, then let out a long breath.

"Okay, Peppernose. I'll be there. Probably should have done this a long time ago. Believe it or not, I don't always know how to be the best mom to you girls I can be. It's not like there's an instruction manual that I can flip to when I get stuck."

"Like an *Idiot-Proof Guide for the Single Mom*?" I said.

Mom took hold of my chin and wiggled it. "You really are a little firecracker, aren't you? Before you go back to school, I'm going to sew a warning label on your shirt. *Danger: Sassy Girl Approaching*."

"Mom!" I yelled, but then we both fell back on the bed laughing. It felt good to laugh like that.

I was a little nervous the next day at school, but the icy fingers left me alone. So did Maddie. She avoided looking at me when she came down the bus aisle. When she and the Oslo twins walked behind me in the hallway, they talked about everything under the sun except me.

I didn't blame Maddie for ignoring me. Coming back to

school must have been harder than anything. She was the perfect girl who wasn't so perfect anymore.

Sometimes, when no one else was looking, I caught sight of her face and briefly glimpsed the scared look in her eyes. Maybe she really wasn't all that different from me, except she had to work harder to hide it.

After all I went through, it would be nice to say I'd sprung out of it like a new butterfly—able to spread my wings, find other butterfly friends, and live happily ever after. But that's not what happened. Most of the time I kept to myself. I was still pretty quiet. I don't think anyone had a clue what had happened to Antonia and me.

Which isn't to say nothing changed. For one thing, I finally agreed to join the after-school art club. When I told May, she wrapped her arms around me and squeezed all the air out of my lungs.

"I knew you'd join, Lucy!" May squealed, grinning so hard I was afraid she might split her face in half. "You are going to love it!"

And she was right. I felt the jitters when I first stepped into Mr. Capp's room, but Mr. Capp welcomed me with his usual smile, and May took hold of my hand and introduced me to the other six kids who'd joined the club. I even cracked a joke about Mr. Capp's mustache, which made everybody laugh. Nobody laughed louder than Mr. Capp.

Then, one day during our regular art class, Mr. Capp

showed me a big book of paintings by an artist named Georgia O'Keeffe. She made gorgeous pictures of flowers and skulls and the New Mexico desert.

"I wish I could paint like her," I said.

Mr. Capp smiled. "You will in your own way. Just keep drawing. Never stop creating beautiful things."

I thought about what Mr. Capp said. The next day I stopped copying pictures out of other books and started drawing what came to mind.

The first thing I drew was the brown face of the Susquehanna River as it flowed past the tall, pale gray birch trees of Hunter's Moon Island.

"You're going to chew that down to your elbow," I said, eyeing the thumbnail Mom was nibbling. Mom pulled it out of her mouth and frowned at it. Then she started working on her pinkie.

Mom had been that way since the volunteer group from Our Lady of the Blessed Sacrament showed up a week after the flood finally receded, offering to clear out the pile of debris that used to be our home. Not that she didn't appreciate it, but church folks always made her twitchy.

Today she was keeping an eye on the man from the Federal Emergency Management Agency who was looking over the broken remains of the trailer. He'd been very friendly and had already assured us we'd almost certainly qualify for home assistance.

That meant we could afford the security deposit on the two-bedroom furnished apartment we'd visited the day before. I had loved it right away. It was roomy and clean, and it had shiny wood floors and a big bay window looking out over the street. Even better, it was only a block away from where May lived.

But none of that kept Mom from trying to gnaw her hand off. Government folks made her even twitchier than church folks.

"I feel like he's judging me," Mom said, who'd moved on to her ring finger.

"Did he say something to you?" I asked.

"No," Mom admitted. "It's just a feeling. Where's Antonia anyway?"

"I'll find her," I said, and ran off toward the road.

I finally found Antonia near the bus stop, but I didn't shout out to her right away. She was talking to Gus Albero. Gus kept his hands stuffed in his front pockets, obviously trying to look cool and collected, and failing miserably. Antonia beamed up at him and bounced on her toes.

Gus spotted me and turned beet red. He said something quickly and scuffled off, his head hanging down like he was willing his neck to swallow it. Antonia turned to me and waved.

"Hey, hey, whaddaya say," she said as she skipped over to me, still beaming.

"Mom's looking for you," I said.

"Sure," Antonia said. I doubt she'd heard a word I said. "Guess what?"

"What?"

"Gus asked me to the Halloween dance!" Antonia smiled so hard I thought she might break all her teeth.

"I thought you weren't talking to him."

"Well, let me tell you what happened." As Antonia started chattering away, I took her by the elbow and led her in Mom's direction. "So I was at my locker yesterday morning and suddenly there's Gus and he says hi but I don't say anything. Then he kind of mumbles, 'Sorry,' and starts looking all stupid and so I kick him."

"You kicked him?"

Antonia nodded like it wasn't such a big deal. "So he's hopping on one foot and he says, 'What did you do that for? I just wanted to ask you to the dance!' And what do you think happened next?"

"You said yes?"

"No!" Antonia squealed. "That weasel face Zoogie pops his ugly head up and starts saying mean things like before, except this time Gus shoves him against the locker and tells him if he says one more word, he's going to be eating fist for lunch." Antonia sighed. "Isn't that the sweetest thing you ever heard?"

I shook my head, but had to smile. I hadn't seen her so happy in a long time.

"That's great," I said, "but good luck trying to get Mom to let you go."

Antonia grabbed my hands. "Can you talk to her, Lucy?" she begged. "You're good at talking to her about things and being convincing. Can you? Please?" She fluttered her eyelashes and puckered her lips like a fish. I laughed and shoved her away.

"All right, I'll see what I can do," I agreed. "But we'd better get back before Mom thinks we both wandered off and got lost again."

We ran, and soon enough we could see the crowd of volunteers sifting through the trailer junk. Mom was listening to the FEMA man while chewing on the one finger that still had a nail. I felt a little winded, so I bent down and put my hands on my knees until I caught my breath.

When I stood up, Antonia was staring wide-eyed with her hand over her mouth.

"What? What is it?" I asked frantically. I felt the icy fingers of panic until I saw the big grin hiding under her hand.

Antonia didn't answer. She took off running, her joyful howler-monkey squeals trailing behind her. She was heading right for the ginkgo tree.

Its leaves had started to fall.

Once I caught up, the two of us just stood there under the branches while the fan-shaped yellow leaves gently floated down and covered our hair and our shoulders and the ground circling our feet. We looked at each other and started to laugh, then we jumped and danced and raced around the tree trunk. Antonia howled and whistled, and I swung my arms out and tried to catch the falling leaves and screamed my head off like a fool.

And I didn't care one bit who heard.

ACKNOWLEDGMENTS

THE ORIGINAL SPARK for *Hush-a-Bye* was a secondhand story I'd heard many years ago. Someone had found a garden gnome's head lying in a creek bed. Five years later, in the very same spot in the creek, they discovered the gnome's body. How I got from that odd little scenario to here was not straightforward or easy, but I do know I did not get here by myself. So I have a few people to thank.

First and foremost is my amazing wife, Suzanne, without whom none of this would have been possible. Her unwavering support for me, despite all the headaches I gave her with my self-doubting rants and obsessive need to find clouds in any silver lining, kept me pushing forward. She is literally (and I do mean *literally*) the best. She is followed closely by my children, Senua and Colin, my parents, my siblings, my in-laws, and all my extended family, who have been there for me for the good days and the difficult ones.

Next, I have to thank my agent, Lindsay Davis Auld, at

Writers House. Lindsay has not only been a steadfast champion for this book since she decided to take me on as a client, but her detailed and incisive notes have made *Hush-a-Bye* a far better book than I had ever imagined. I feel like I am a better writer now because of her, which is no small thing.

Thanks also to everyone at Viking Children's Books/Penguin Random House who helped in getting this book together. In particular, I'd like to thank my editor, Jenny Bak, for her guidance and her keen editorial eye, and for just being an engaging person with whom I've enjoyed working. And special thanks to illustrator and apparent mind reader Matt Rockfeller for creating the cover I'd always imagined.

Thanks as well to a group of wonderful writers—Margaret Peterson Haddix, Lesa Cline-Ransome, Kat Shepherd, and Christina Uss—whom I've had the pleasure to talk to about children's books, and who graciously agreed to read my manuscript and offer their generous feedback.

A shout-out of thanks to New York West/Central chapter of SCBWI New York, whose conferences and critique sessions helped me hone my craft. A special shout-out to Darcy Pattison and the Novel Revision retreat she helmed, which did so much to bring focus to the book's shape, as well as the middle grade group who offered their insightful suggestions: Rinda Beach, Kim Gillett, Susan Tabriz, and Kim Jakaway.

And going way back, a big thanks to the online group Critique Circle and those fellow writers who provided such smart critiques to the very earliest drafts of the book, with special mention going to T. J. McIntosh, Molly Zucknick, and Linda Kelly.

And finally, I'd like to offer my gratitude to the great writer Shirley Jackson. She sustained me through high school with her strange, mesmerizing stories of lost and wounded people, and I hope this book might do the same for any reader looking for a port in the storm, even if for only a little while.

ABOUT THE AUTHOR

JODY LEE MOTT is a former elementary and middle school teacher, and an avid reader of children's books who finally decided to write down the stories bouncing around his brain. He is also the creator and host of the children's book podcast *Dream Gardens*, which is on Stitcher, Spotify, and wherever podcasts are found. He lives several stone throws from the Susquehanna River in Apalachin, New York, with his wife, children, and one very large greyhound. *Hush-a-Bye* is his first novel. Find him at jodyleemott.com.